Hilary looked unconvinced

"I still feel like such a washout. I'm not sure I'll ever be able to get my confidence back."

"Don't say that," Rick said gruffly. "I'll help you." He wouldn't stop until he succeeded. Knowing there was only one way to convince her of that, he bent and touched his lips to hers, and once he'd tasted the sweetness of her mouth, he couldn't get enough of her. Even as she submitted to his need, she demanded.

Wild, passionate thoughts exploded in his head. Her mouth seemed fused to his. He began to feel and see the layers of mystery, the depth of the woman inside, to have a sense of how she could give and give. And he knew then how much he needed her, the loving spirit that belonged to Hilary and Hilary alone.

ABOUT THE AUTHOR

Cathy Gillen Thacker has been writing for years under her own name and pseudonyms. Besides writing warm family stories for Harlequin American Romance, she has written several romantic suspenses. Cathy got into writing in a roundabout way. After attending Miami University she taught piano to children, while turning to romance fiction. She now resides with her husband and children in Texas, where she continues to draw on her experiences to create warm, realistic stories.

Books by Cathy Gillen Thacker

HARLEQUIN AMERICAN ROMANCE

262–NATURAL TOUCH
277–PERFECT MATCH
307–ONE MAN'S FOLLY
318–LIFETIME GUARANTEE
334–MEANT TO BE

HARLEQUIN TEMPTATION

47–EMBRACE ME, LOVE
82–A PRIVATE PASSION

HARLEQUIN INTRIGUE

94–FATAL AMUSEMENT
104–DREAM SPINNERS
137–SLALOM TO TERROR

CATHY GILLEN THACKER

IT'S ONLY TEMPORARY

Harlequin Books

TORONTO • NEW YORK • LONDON
AMSTERDAM • PARIS • SYDNEY • HAMBURG
STOCKHOLM • ATHENS • TOKYO • MILAN

Published November 1990

ISBN 0-373-16367-3

Chapter One

Hilary Morgan knew the moment she walked in the door that the chief of staff had bad news for her. She took the seat the older woman indicated, bracing herself for the worst. As she expected, the ax wasn't long in coming.

"I'm sorry, Dr. Morgan, but the medical review board's decision is final," Dr. Lynn Whitfield said. "You're suspended from the hospital until the malpractice case against you is resolved."

Hilary had known this was coming; there was no real reason for her to feel so surprised or devastated. But she did, maybe because there was no way to prepare for such a blow. Needing a moment to compose herself, she directed her gaze past the polished wood and marble interior of the administrator's office, to the window beyond. Outdoors, century-old elms and magnolias bloomed with the vigor of late spring. In Boston's famed Public Garden, flowers bloomed luxuriantly. Brightly colored sailboats filled the harbor and the Red Sox played in Fenway Park, while here and now her own life was falling apart with terrifying speed.

It had started months ago, when she had taken on a new patient. A chemistry professor at MIT, Mrs. Jones had been in her late thirties and was the kind of patient who thought she already knew everything. Hilary hadn't really minded her know-it-all attitude. She simply counseled her as she would any other new patient and asked her to come back in four weeks for her second prenatal checkup.

Unfortunately Mrs. Jones put off that appointment, rescheduling twice. Finally, near the end of her third month, she came in again. Hilary checked her and she was fine. Although Hilary could tell Mrs. Jones considered the routine monthly visits unnecessary, she cautioned her anyway on the importance of them. Her talk served little purpose. Mrs. Jones missed her next appointment, too. When she finally came in again, this time halfway into her fifth month, Hilary examined her and found nothing amiss. Figuring it wouldn't do much good to lecture her patient again, she said nothing about the missed appointments. The exam ended on a cordial note. The next time she saw Mrs. Jones was several days later in the emergency room.

Mrs. Jones's cervix had opened and she'd miscarried. She had been very distraught over the loss of her baby, and so had Hilary, although her medical training had kept her from showing it at the time. She kept thinking, wondering, going back over the case in her mind, trying to figure out if maybe there had been something she'd missed. But she hadn't come up with anything, and knowing they had to put this behind them and move on, she had composed herself and gone on to explain to Mrs. Jones that she had an incompetent cervix and now that they knew that, there were things they could do the next time she was pregnant. They could surgically sew the cervix shut, give her some medicine and so forth to keep her from miscarrying. Mrs. Jones had seemed to accept that.

Hilary had thought everything was fine. The next thing she had known she'd been slapped with a malpractice suit for ten million dollars, for the loss of Mrs. Jones's baby. Hilary had been devastated then, and she was still reeling from the shock of it and her own residual feelings of guilt and inadequacy.

"You understand suspending you wasn't my choice," her superior said gently, bringing her back into the present. "But with the civil trial pending against you, the hospital's insurance company refuses to grant malpractice insurance coverage for you in the area of obstetrics and gynecology—at any fee."

The situation was beyond her, Hilary thought with a beleaguered sigh, since Massachusetts already had one of the highest malpractice fees for obstetrics in the nation. Had they chosen to continue to insure her, she would have had to pay upwards of two hundred thousand dollars a year, just for the privilege of practicing medicine. It was incredible. It was highway robbery. And yet knowing the outlandish size of some of the jury awards to litigants, Hilary could well understand why the nervous insurance companies were compelled to charge so much. Physicians had to be responsible, and patients' rights safeguarded. And the insurance companies had to be prepared to pay out millions of dollars in malpractice cases every year, as in the one against her.

"The hospital therefore can't let you admit any OB/GYN patients or practice in the hospital," Dr. Whitfield continued.

A thought came to her. "What about in the area of general medicine?"

"The hospital's medical review board would prefer you wait on that—at least here—until your situation is resolved."

Or in other words, they didn't want to run the risk of a second malpractice case lodged against her before the first was settled, Hilary realized, disappointed.

"Perhaps if you were to look elsewhere—away from Boston," Dr. Whitfield suggested kindly.

She had a point. What few patients Hilary had had after the news of the lawsuit broke, had been scared away by the adverse publicity and allegations of gross incompetence. Allegations Hilary even now was hard-pressed to deny. Had it been her fault Mrs. Jones had lost her baby? She didn't want to think so, but she also knew Mrs. Jones had miscarried during a particularly hectic two-week period in which Hilary had done five C-sections—two of which had been emergencies. She'd also presided over a dozen other births, plus carried her full patient load. As thorough and alert as she'd tried to be, there was a chance she had been overtired and accidentally missed signs of an impending second-trimester miscarriage in the equally harried MIT professor.

A very bright, impatient and self-contained woman, Mrs. Jones had not been prone to complain about anything. Nor had she seen fit to reveal much about herself of a personal nature in the few minutes Hilary'd been with her. Initially Hilary had respected Mrs. Jones's wish to be examined and then left alone, but now she wished she had taken the time and initiative to get to know her patient better. Maybe if she had, Mrs. Jones would have listened to her and not taken those routine visits so lightly. Maybe she would have felt freer to discuss any seemingly "minor" aches or twinges she'd been having with Hilary. And maybe Hilary would have identified those twinges as a sign of trouble and acted accordingly. But she hadn't gotten close to her patient when she'd had the chance, and now it was too late. Nothing could ever bring Mrs. Jones's baby back...or mitigate Hilary's personal sorrow over the loss.

"How long before the case comes to court?" Dr. Whitfield asked, her calm, practical voice drawing Hilary's thoughts back to the present.

"Six months."

"That long?" Dr. Whitfield looked disturbed.

Hilary sighed. *She wants this over, too.* "My lawyer, Dash Barrington, has been trying to get an earlier date, so has the attorney for the insurance company, but you know how backlogged the courts are."

Silence fell between them. "Do you have any thoughts about what you're going to do in the meantime?" Dr. Whitfield prodded.

"The job offers haven't exactly been pouring in." She looked at Dr. Whitfield hopefully. "Any suggestions as to where I might try?"

"Well, there is an opening for a general physician in rural Kentucky. I just heard about the position opening up yesterday, so I doubt it's been filled yet." Rifling through the correspondence on her desk, she finally located the paper she wanted. "The job pays twenty-eight thousand a year, and is under the auspices of the county public-health bureau. There are a few perks—a house and transportation are provided. The physician's medical-malpractice insurance premiums are paid by the government." She glanced up with an encouraging smile. "You know one of the other physicians working in the area—a Dr. Rick

Burnett. He did his residency at Boston General, too, about the time you did yours, I believe."

Hilary had never really gotten to know Rick; their paths had crossed infrequently because they were always in different rotations. She remembered him as tall and rugged, a native of rural Kentucky who had intended to go back to the family and fiancée he had waiting for him there. But that was about all she knew about him, beside the fact he'd had a positive reputation among the staff.

"Appalachia...I don't know. I've always been a city person." To be perfectly honest, the thought of living in the backwoods of Kentucky, never mind working there for any length of time, thoroughly unnerved her. Yet staying on in Massachusetts had no more appeal, because she would have to work under the cloud of the lawsuit. After nearly two months of dealing with it, she was tired of talking about the situation, tired of worrying about what was going to happen to her, tired of feeling half ill with guilt and stress all the time. If she went to Kentucky, she reasoned slowly, no one would have to know what had happened with Mrs. Jones and her baby. She wouldn't have to face the constant gossip, the doubts. She wouldn't have to feel constantly on edge. She could concentrate on medicine again, try and get her confidence back. Try to make up in some way for what she'd done—or more precisely hadn't done, for Mrs. Jones. And doing that had to be better than sitting here idle, letting all her twelve years of extensive education and medical training go to waste.

"I won't kid you. According to the letter from Rick, this is no easy job. If you decide to take it you'll have to go on house calls, because a lot of the people you'll be seeing don't have any transportation of their own. Plus the medical equipment they have is not the best, not anything near what you're accustomed to here at Boston General. It'll be tough for you, an adjustment, but on the other hand by going there I think you could learn a lot and certainly see things you wouldn't see anywhere else in this country." Dr. Whitfield paused, then finished persuasively, "It could be a real learning experience for you, Hilary."

There was no denying she could use a change, or that she'd much rather be thousands of miles from Boston, away from the reporters and the innuendo, Hilary thought. Away from her own doubts about her abilities as a physician. Doubts that had started way before she ever went to med school, when she was a kid. When her younger sister was still alive.... That day still haunted Hilary. She and Marcy had been outside playing, when a bee stung Marcy. Hilary had applied a compress. But before long, swelling began—an intense allergic reaction to the sting. Hilary immediately called for an ambulance, but it was too late before the medics arrived. The agony, the fear, the helplessness still made Hilary awaken at night in a cold sweat.

The tragedy had led to Hilary's decision to enter medical school. She never again wanted to feel that helpless. Yet here she was in a similar situation.

With effort, she pushed the tumultuous emotions from her mind. "Does Rick work for the same setup?" she asked, aware her voice had started to tremble slightly as she considered the possibility of going to work again.

Her boss nodded. "Rick not only works there, he's the lead physician in a three-county area. From what I understand, they've got two physicians per county. All the slots are filled except the one in Rick's county."

"Would I work with Rick directly?" And if so, how bossy would he be? Would he insist she do everything his way and his way alone? Somehow, she thought not. She thought he'd give her space. But was space what she wanted? She'd been so nervous of late, to be there on unfamiliar turf, without the high-tech hospital backup she was used to...she wasn't sure she could handle too much on her own, especially at first.

"In the beginning, yes, you'd work for Rick since he is the lead physician, then later probably mostly on your own. Rick indicated in his letter that they needed a physician badly. I think you would have a good chance of getting it, despite your professional problems."

Hilary paused. That was probably true. Not many physicians would want a position in rural Appalachia. The question was, did she really want the job? Was it worth the risk and hardship involved?

RICK BURNETT PROPPED his feet on the corner of his scarred maple desk and studied the file in front of him. He'd been surprised to see Hilary Morgan's name put in for the county-physician job. He remembered her as a very pretty, very citified woman who had a knack for fashion and theater. She was hardly the type to be out driving alone in the backwoods, catering to patients one-on-one. No, Hilary Morgan belonged in a modern hospital, in sterile scrubs, surrounded by high-tech equipment and first-rate help. And she had been, until disaster had struck in the form of the malpractice suit recently filed against her.

Hearing about it, he'd immediately felt for her. Even though he'd only known her from a distance she'd always seemed so dedicated, and he knew just from the fact she'd been accepted into Boston General's ultraselective residency program that she was smart, gifted, extremely well-educated. While he was in Boston, she'd done extremely well.

Yet barely a year into private practice, things had gone dreadfully wrong for her. Although he suspected the case against her was overblown, it would be months resolving. Hence, she was now looking for a place to wait out the difficulties up north, a place where she could still practice. He didn't have any question about her ability; he knew in his gut she was highly competent, and that time would bear out his opinion. He did, however, worry about her ability to adapt.

If it weren't for the fact they needed a doctor badly, particularly one with obstetrical skills, he would've been tempted to keep looking. He preferred a physician from rural Kentucky, someone who would unquestionably and immediately understand the people, their way of life. But he knew his chance of finding someone in a crunch was next to nil.

In the two months he'd posted the job, he'd only had one applicant—Hilary—and experience told him there were none likely to follow soon.

His thoughts roved back to Hilary Morgan. He'd always found her attractive—with her soft shoulder-length black hair and her dark blue eyes—but he didn't really know her in a personal sense. During residency, they'd both been too intent on finishing up and pursuing their separate goals—big city for her, the country for him—to get better acquainted.

Rick sighed and ran a hand wearily over his eyes, feeling exhausted from yet another eighteen-hour day. God knew he couldn't go on like this, stretched to the maximum much longer. They needed another doctor here, and now.

Maybe Hilary could be happy for a year or so, he thought, if he and his family went out of their way to help her adjust. Certainly, it was worth a try. Later if she decided, as he half suspected she would, that she

wanted to leave, then he'd accept that and wish her
well. In the meantime he'd get some temporary help...
He'd get to know Hilary, as he never had been able to
when he was in Boston. It wasn't the optimum situation, but it was all he had right now. He would settle
for that and hope for a whole lot more.

A DOZEN TIMES over the course of the next few days,
Hilary had a chance to regret her impetuous decision
to accept Rick Burnett's job offer. What did she know
about country medicine? What did she know about
living in the country, period? Yet knowing she had no
choice, that she had to get away from the stress and
turmoil in Boston, kept her going. Somehow she
would find a way to make this work for however long
she needed it to, Hilary schooled herself firmly.

Nonetheless, a feeling nagged. The people in the
Lexington terminal seemed so different somehow, so
provincial. All except Rick. In the three years since
they had seen one another, he hadn't changed. He was
still slim and rangy, with thick wheat-blond hair forever in need of a cut, and mesmerizing silver-gray eyes.
His button-fly Levi's were so old the seams were almost white, the fabric washed to a light blue, yet on
him the snug-fitting pants were exactly right. His blue
chambray shirt was clean and rumpled and open at the
throat. His buff-colored boots were polished to a soft
shine. He'd always had a lazy, predatory grace, but
now as he threaded his way through the crowd to her

side, he was even more at ease and self-assured than he
had been in Boston.

His eyes met hers and stayed. Her spirits plum-
meted when she saw the doubt in his eyes. He knows,
she thought. He's wondering if I'm guilty, too.

"How was the flight?"

It was a simple question, his attitude one of genial
cordiality; there was no reason her throat should feel
so dry. Yet she persisted in feeling as awkward and ill-
at-ease as a teenager on her first day of high school.
Maybe because he was so appealing in his own rugged, laid-back way. "Uneventful, thanks."

Frowning slightly, he slid a hand beneath her elbow
and guided her out of the way of an oncoming throng
of weary travelers. His touch was warm and gently
protecting, there was no reason she should be so aware
of him. Yet she was. "Ready to head out, or do you
want to stop and get something to eat?"

Now that she was here, she wanted to see where she
would be living and working. Anything to get her
mind off Rick. She lifted her chin resolutely. "I had
breakfast on the plane, so . . . let's go."

They got her two suitcases and proceeded to the
parking lot. Rick insisted on helping, so she was left
carrying just her medical bag, her purse and the stack
of magazines she'd bought to read on the plane.
Hilary, feeling a little warm in the muggy June air,
took off her suit jacket and slung it over her arm. His
gaze slid over her white silk shirt and slim navy skirt,

lingering a moment on her narrow waist before returning to her flushed face with ease. "A little warmer than you're used to?" he asked kindly.

She figured it had to be ninety in the shade. But she also knew she'd feel better when she got inside an air-conditioned car. "Slightly, but I'll survive," she said drily.

He nodded and continued, not breaking stride. Adjusting the length of his longer steps to her shorter ones, he stopped in front of a beat-up black pickup truck that had to be at least fifteen years old. The whole underside was coated with rust; over that was a thick layer of dust. She didn't need to ask, to know that this back-to-basics model had no air-conditioning. "Did the county provide your truck, too?" she asked, almost afraid to hear the answer.

Rick grinned. "Yep. You'll get one, too."

One sentence had never sounded so devastating. Fighting a sinking feeling, Hilary took a deep, bolstering breath and got in the truck. It rumbled and groaned before it finally started.

Listening to the protesting engine, she wanted to turn around then and there. He looked at her and laughed. He shook his head in silent remonstration. "Relax. You'll—"

"Get used to it, I know," she finished, in chorus with him.

His silver eyes glinted at her from beneath the shock of wheat-colored hair. "I'll be around to help you," he soothed lazily.

She had no doubt of that, either. Somehow, though, it didn't seem as comforting a thought now as it had back in Boston. Maybe because she was achingly aware of how good he smelled in the unair-conditioned cab of the truck, like pine trees deep in the forest. Whereas she, feeling grubby after a long flight that had required her to switch planes at La Guardia, wanted only to relax in a long, hot bubble bath, liberally scented with White Linen. Well, she'd have her chance, as soon as they arrived.

Concentrating on that, she stared out the window at the passing scenery. To her delight, the city seemed to have a charm of its own. There were plenty of immaculately kept horse farms, fencing in miles of pastures filled with sleek brown horses. Thirty or more miles out of Lexington, the horse farms that had been so prominent grew sparser. The rolling hills and heavily treed areas increased, and they climbed steadily, going from Lexington's nine-hundred-eighty-three-foot elevation to over two thousand feet. As they left the main highway and turned onto a roughly paved two-lane road, the few towns they passed consisted of no more than a one-room general store and a gas station. She saw an occasional small school, and every great once in a while a funeral home or a church. That was about it.

"I take it this is our territory," she said after a while, privately depressed at the sights around them.

"You guessed right," Rick said, slanting her a glance. His look narrowed even more. She knew he was testing her, trying to get a more personal reaction from her.

She kept her face expressionless and determined not to give it to him. If he was trying to see how tough she could be, then she wouldn't disappoint him. They rode on in stoic silence. She thought, but couldn't be sure, that after a few minutes, his mouth began to curve approvingly again.

Finally, some fifteen more miles and no cities later, Rick turned the truck down a long, tree-lined drive. At first, Hilary was hopeful the house would be as beautiful as the land it was built on, with its abundance of maple, hickory and walnut trees, flowering lilac bushes and the occasional elm. No such luck, she realized with a sinking feeling as they reached the end of the lane.

The house was small, as was the lean-to shed behind it. A few flakes of aging yellow paint littered the lawn, but for the most part the wood exterior was bare. Two rotting steps led up to a small porch. The screen door hung off its hinges. A torn, crooked shade hung over one window. The other was bare.

Rick cut the motor.

The silence between them was devastating. Hilary didn't know whether to cry or laugh, but she could tell by the look on Rick's face that this, indeed, was it. Her house. Her home for the next six months. Oh, Lord, what had she gotten herself into now? she wondered.

Rick jumped down from the truck. She followed behind him feeling a little sick and dizzy from the rough ride they'd just had over the narrow curving country roads, and the shock she'd just been dealt.

Frowning, but not bothering to explain his mood, Rick bounded lightly up the steps. Reaching into his pocket, he produced a key and unlocked the front door.

Inside was even worse than she had imagined. There were two very small rooms and a bath, and they were covered with layers of dust and grime. Cobwebs hung from the ceiling. The sturdy dinette set was old and scratched. The coffee tables weren't in much better shape, and the vinyl sofa with one leg broken off tilted to the right. Trash was strewn everywhere, as if the prior occupant had left in a hurry.

Rick sighed and rested both his hands on his hips. "This was supposed to be cleaned before you got here."

Frankly, Hilary wasn't sure a simple cleaning would help. Her quarters were so much less than what she had expected. Before she had a chance to comment, another truck barreled up the lane and came to an abrupt halt.

She turned to see a plump, pleasant-looking woman get out of a brand new red-and-gray Ford pickup truck. The woman waved at the two of them, and lifted a bucket of cleaning supplies and a mop from the truck bed. She was dressed in jeans and a long, loose red gingham shirt that reached halfway down her ample hips.

"You must be the new doctor," she called out cheerily as she dashed up the steps, successfully side-stepping the rotted wood with barely a passing glance. "Hilary, isn't it?" The older woman with the curly gray-brown hair pumped Hilary's hand vigorously. "I'm Rick's mom, Alva. And I'm pleased to meet you."

"It's nice to meet you," Hilary said, looking into the woman's twinkling light blue eyes and thinking she'd found at least one friend already, besides Rick. She began to relax. Maybe this wouldn't be so bad after all. Once she got the place cleaned up, she could relax.

Alva sent her an apologetic glance. "I meant to get this done before you arrived, but I've been busy planning my other son's wedding...I'm also sewing my future daughter-in-law's wedding gown...the time just got away from me. I hope you can forgive me."

"There's nothing to forgive." Hilary smiled. "And you don't have to worry about helping me clean. I can do it." She'd never been afraid of a little hard work, and maybe it was good the local people see that from the start. She didn't want people thinking they had to wait on her hand and foot. She was here to do a job, to bring medical care to people who wouldn't otherwise have any.

Rick looked at her with new respect, obviously relieved she was taking this all so well. "You're sure?" he said tactfully.

Hilary nodded, determined to make this house her own no matter how much scrubbing it took. She was here, she would make the best of it. "I'm sure," she said firmly, meeting his gaze. Besides, she'd always found something very cathartic in hard work. "I'm going to need some supplies. And food." She glanced at the bare socket overhead. "Light bulbs. Is the electricity turned on?"

Rick went over and tried it. Nothing. He sighed again. "Electrical service is notoriously slow out here, but I'll go into town and see what I can do about getting the electricity turned on ASAP."

Normally Hilary liked to fight her own battles, but this was one she would willingly let him handle for her. She looked at Alva. "Would you mind if I borrowed your cleaning supplies?"

"Not at all. You don't want me to stay and help?" Alva asked. She already had her sleeves rolled up, and looked raring to go.

If I'm going to fit in here, she thought, I have to make friends. And the truth was, she could use a helping hand, even though she felt a little awkward accepting it. "Actually, I'd like that very much," Hilary said.

"Great. I'll get the rest of the supplies from the truck and then we can get started," Alva said. Although the chore ahead of them was gargantuan, she looked incredibly happy, as if Hilary had just made her day.

"I'll head into town and get some food for you and some light bulbs," Rick said. He consulted his watch. "I've got a few patients to check on, but I'll stop back later on. Maybe about six."

Hilary nodded. Six it would be.

After Rick left, Hilary changed into jeans and an old Yale sweatshirt left over from her college days. While Alva swept out the floors and scrubbed the dickens out of the bathroom, Hilary gathered up all the trash, carried it outside, and then attacked the cobwebs inside. Armed with buckets of hot water and Murphy's wood soap, Hilary went to work on the wooden floors and furniture. Alva turned to the kitchen cupboards, cleaning them thoroughly inside and out. Hilary took down the window shades and cleaned the glass until it shined. "You know," Alva said thoughtfully, staring at the café-curtain rods hanging above the windows. "I've got some ruffled white curtains at home that would probably fit. They're just sitting in my linen closet. Want me to go and get them?"

As she hadn't been looking forward to tacking sheets up over the windows, Hilary nodded vigorously. The idea was splendid.

While Alva was gone, Hilary got to work on the inside of the ancient refrigerator, simultaneously cleaning and disinfecting it with a solution of bleach and water. She'd nearly finished when she heard a truck in the drive. Expecting to see Alva, she got up and went to the front door. Instead she saw Rick coming her way, a sack of groceries in one hand, a toolbox in the other. "Figured I'd fix your screen door while I'm here," he said, handing her the groceries. She was a little disappointed to see there was only fresh fruit, a jar of peanut butter and a loaf of bread inside. "The electricity won't be turned on until tomorrow," he said apologetically. "I had to pull some strings to manage even that. I'm sorry."

"It's okay," Hilary heard herself saying, although inwardly her heart was sinking. How was she going to live without electricity? Without lights?

"At any rate, Mom figured you'd be hungry for some real food and she sent over some dinner. She included those curtains she promised you." He headed back to the truck.

When he returned he was armed with a huge wicker picnic basket and a thermal jug equipped with a pouring spout. The smells coming from the basket were tantalizing: Hilary opened the top to find a platter full of crispy fried chicken, hot and fresh buttermilk biscuits, homemade strawberry jam in a mason jar. There were also fresh green beans flavored with little bits of country ham, and garden-fresh carrots, and cucumbers sliced ready to eat.

Rick stayed and ate with her, the two of them sitting on the porch. By the time they'd finished, the sun had started to fall beyond the horizon.

"That was the best meal I've had in ages," Hilary said, meaning it. She polished off another glass of icy lemonade.

"I'll tell Mom you liked it," he grinned back, resting against one of the four beams that supported the porch.

In the dwindling light, the country seemed very peaceful. And Rick—very dangerous. The new tension that had sprung up between them was not something either of them wanted. Yes, he was a very attractive man, but the attraction wasn't something she could or would act on.

"I better get those curtains, if we want to get them hung before dark," he said, pushing to his feet. "Mom sent some bed sheets and clean towels, too. She said you can borrow them as long as you like, or till your own linens arrive."

To Hilary's relief Rick was all business when he returned from the truck, and the process of hanging the curtains went swiftly. When they'd finished Hilary looked around, satisfied. The place wasn't half bad, now that she'd gotten it cleaned up. It was still primitive, of course, but she wouldn't be here forever, a fact that consoled her immeasurably.

"Ready to go on rounds with me tomorrow morning?" he asked, his manner solely that of one doctor to another.

Now that I'm here, I might as well dig in. Although exhaustion was already beginning to kick in, she braced herself and gave him a cheerful smile. "Sure. What time?"

"I'll pick you up around eight," he said casually. "That okay with you?"

"Sure." Aware of the pulse beating erratically in her throat, she smiled at him again. Hands in her pockets, she walked him out to the truck. Because he was taller than she by a good six or eight inches, she had to tilt her head back to look up into his eyes. "When exactly am I going to be getting that transportation of my own I was promised?" she asked. The sooner she was independent and could stop relying on him, the better.

He shifted the wicker basket in his hands, reaching into his jeans pockets for his keys. He sucked in his lower abdomen slightly as he drew them out, making her aware of just how flat his stomach was.

He sorted through the keys on the ring until he found the appropriate one. "Your truck's being worked on over at Harper's filling station. Should be ready in another couple of days." He opened the door and slid the basket in across the seat, then leaned over to settle it securely on the floor of the passenger side.

She was almost afraid to ask what was wrong with her truck. Some things, she figured, were better not knowing. Besides, she'd had enough shocks for one day. "Okay. Thanks for dinner, all the help," she said.

He smiled again, looking cheerful. "Any time. I mean that." Briefly, his eyes held hers with mesmerizing intensity.

Discomfited by the gentleness she saw in his kind and handsome face, she turned away. Not only was she beginning to like this place but she was beginning to like him. And that wouldn't do. She'd be leaving and they were colleagues, after all . . .

Turning, she started back toward the house. She'd gotten no farther than four or five steps when she saw it, a slim gray body rustling beneath the ragged green-and-lavender branches of an overgrown lilac bush and darting behind the crumbling front steps. She wasn't sure what it was; she only knew it was big—at least a foot long—and furry, with some sort of long, swishing tail.

Terrified, she stumbled backward and let out a startled cry that echoed in the dusky light. Whatever was beneath the shadowy confines of the porch rustled again, louder this time, and then seemed to approach her. Hilary didn't wait around—she wasn't about to stand there and get bitten. Heaven only knew what kind of diseases the wild animal carried. Pivoting, still shaking with fright, she broke into a hard, fast run up the steps and slammed the door.

No electricity, and gray creatures under the porch. She'd have a hard night ahead.

Fortunately Rick had started a fire. If necessary, she'd stay up and stoke it all night.

Chapter Two

The next morning Rick was back as promised. He was surprised not to find Hilary waiting on the front porch. Then again this was her first night in Appalachia, he reminded himself. Without electricity, she might have been scared and experienced a restless night. The fire would have helped there. Darn it, if she weren't so independent, he'd have taken her home last night to Alva.

Indeed when he knocked, it was a while before the door opened. Confronting him was a bedraggled, tired Hilary. "Bad night?"

She frowned at him. "These are not exactly the conditions I'm used to living in. Besides, just as you left last night I discovered there's a r-r-rat's nest under the porch!"

He glanced at her disbelievingly. "Are you sure?"

She nodded.

"Stay here. I'll check it out." Still shaking his head in a mixture of bewilderment and disbelief, he proceeded confidently down the steps to his truck and returned with a flashlight.

"Squirrels," he pronounced, after a few moments of intense inspection. "There's a big nest of them down there. They probably wintered there the last year or two. Maybe longer." He stood and flicked the light off. His amused grin widened. "You didn't hear them earlier, when you were cleaning?"

Hilary shook her head, not knowing whether to laugh or cry. Suddenly, it seemed, her legs would barely support her.

Aware her adrenaline was spent, as were her nerves, she steadied herself by touching a hand to the rock solidness of his chest. With effort, she slowed the frantic thudding of her heart.

"It's okay," Rick said, setting a shielding arm about her waist. "Last night was a rude welcome. You're just a little green yet. You'll adjust to the rigors of country life."

Without warning, her chin lifted and she straightened.

"Boston has its own share of hardships. Believe me, when I first arrived there I had plenty to master."

Her brows drew together in surprise. "Such as?"

"The subway. I'd never been on one. And the food. I hated cod, and I never cared much for their baked beans, either," Rick continued.

"But you adjusted?" asked Hilary.

He nodded, and smiled, his silver eyes softening her until she leaned into him even more. "Maybe in time you'll learn to love Kentucky, too. But in the meantime there's no reason for you to play hostess to a family of Kentucky squirrels. I'll get my younger brother to come over first thing this afternoon and send them packing. He'll board the space up nice and tight so they can't get in again." He looked her up and down. Without warning, he frowned. His eyes took on a serious cast. "You know what?" he drawled, the arm he had anchored about her waist tightening protectively. "You don't look too good."

As it happened, she felt a little dizzy, like she was about to collapse from sheer exhaustion—both physical and emotional. "I suppose I have looked better."

"Tell you what," he said, his arm urging her toward the truck. "What if I take you home, so you can wash up and have a bite to eat?"

Although clearly tempted to give in, she resisted him. "What about the patients?"

He shrugged. "I'll call our morning appointments and let them know we'll be late."

Hearing the sense in his words, Hilary smiled. "Lead the way, Dr. Burnett."

To her delight, his mother's house was a pleasing surprise. A narrow three-story farmhouse built somewhere near the turn of the century, it was painted a slate-blue color, with white scalloped gingerbread trim adorning the eaves and edges of the roof. The windows had white shutters. The porch hosted window boxes filled with flowers. His mother's shiny new pickup truck was parked in the gravel drive alongside the house.

Alva was already up and in the kitchen when Rick led Hilary in. Fortunately he was sensitive enough to her feelings of awkwardness and unkemptness to take her to an upstairs bathroom. She could clean up while Rick explained the situation and called patients.

BY THE TIME she got back downstairs thirty minutes later, Alva was breaking eggs into a pan. "Coffee's ready," Alva called cheerily, pointing to the wooden rack where mugs were kept. "Help yourself. How do you like your eggs?"

"Over easy, please," Hilary said. She looked around with pleasure. Alva's kitchen, like something out of a Norman Rockwell painting, was cozy and cluttered, the appliances old-fashioned but well-scrubbed.

Momentarily she reflected back on her own youth. She had few memories of her mother—who'd died when she was six. After that, they'd always had housekeepers to do the cooking and cleaning. Her father had been a traveling salesman for a pharmaceutical company and had been home very little of the time. He had been there even less frequently after her sister died.

Alva smiled at her warmly. "It'll be about fifteen minutes before the eggs are ready. Would you like some juice?"

Hilary saw the pitcher on the table. "I'll get it. Thanks." Still feeling weighted down by sleep, she watched as Alva shaped biscuit dough between the flats of her palms and then placed the fluffy rounds on a baking tray.

"So how did you sleep?" Alva asked, sliding two dozen biscuits into the oven to bake.

"Fairly well," Hilary lied. When she had dozed off she'd dreamed about Rick and gray furry creatures, her sister's death and the lawsuit still pending against her in Boston. It wasn't exactly a nightmare, more a collage of her life that didn't make any sense. Only the parts with Rick in them had been the least bit realistic, and in fact, those parts had been almost too realistic because they'd left her feeling incomplete.

At that moment, the back door slammed. Rick walked in, looking energetic and ready to go. He moved around to give his mom a kiss and then poured himself some coffee. For the second time that day, Hilary found herself glad to be with him.

"Well, everyone knows we'll be an hour late."

"Well, don't just stand there," Alva murmured teasingly. "Your food's waiting."

Breakfast was delicious. They were almost through when Rick asked his mom, "Kenny home?"

"He's already gone to work, but I asked him about the squirrels. He said he'd take care of it this afternoon, just as soon as he finished bush-hogging the fields for the Whittingtons." Alva looked at Hilary. "Kenny hires out for a lot of farm work, here and there. He's been working especially hard lately, because he and Daisy need every penny they can get."

Rick frowned, and got up to pour himself more coffee.

He remained uncommonly quiet as Alva filled Hilary in on Kenny's wedding plans. Hilary wondered at Rick's disinterest in the details of his brother's upcoming nuptials. Was it because he didn't care about such things in general, or because he didn't approve of the wedding? She sensed a tenseness in him during the talk.

When they stepped outside half an hour later, the morning was fresh and clear and cool. Hilary took a deep breath, appreciating everything about the quiet countryside, from the soft chirping of the birds to the absence of traffic sounds.

Rick circled to his side of the truck, while Hilary climbed into the passenger side. "So where are we going first?" she asked.

He slid behind the wheel and shut the door. "The coal mine. We go there once a week to look after the miners. They get routine physicals and treatment for any health problems that have cropped up. You'll never get a more vivid look at Appalachia than there. It's as good a place as any to start.''

Was it? Hilary felt a now-familiar knot of anxiety in the pit of her stomach. Since the Jones case, she had been plagued with doubts about her ability to accurately diagnose ailments. She was dismayed to find her unfamiliar surroundings, coupled with her foray back into general medicine, only exacerbated that fear. Taking a deep breath, she forced herself to relax and concentrate on what Rick was saying about the range of mining operations in the state.

Fifteen minutes later, they arrived at their destination.

Going on into the mining-company office, he greeted the workers inside with the ease of someone who has long been accepted in the community. Her heart pumping adrenaline at a breakneck rate, Hilary wasn't really surprised to find she was greeted less cordially. After all, he was the old-timer, she the newcomer to the area.

"You're a doctor?" one of the women working in the office said, looking at her with unbridled skepticism.

"Yes." Hilary forced a smile anyway. She'd braced herself for a lot of things, but hadn't figured on encountering prejudice against her gender.

Fortunately another woman with straight, light brown hair, closely cropped, said, "And it's about time we had a woman in this part of Kentucky. Hello," she extended her hand. "I'm Emma Schwartz. I work for the EPA. It's nice to meet you. You've got a definite New England accent there."

Hilary noted reflexively that Emma was about five months pregnant, judging by the rounded silhouette beneath the blue maternity smock and elastic-waist jeans. She seemed healthy enough, if a bit bloated. Turning her mind back to Emma's inquiry, Hilary said, "I'm originally from Boston."

Emma's brows raised. She continued politely, "You went to school there, too?"

Hilary nodded, aware she was beginning to get uncomfortable. She didn't want anyone delving too closely into her past, for fear they would find out why she'd had to leave Boston so unexpectedly. She'd lose their trust, and hence, her effectiveness. "Yale for my B.S. and Harvard Med for my M.D."

Emma's brows rose another notch as she gave Hilary a very thorough—and Hilary couldn't help but think critical—once-over. "I'm impressed." She looked at Rick, sensed his unusual fidgetiness, and then back at Hilary. "What brought you here?"

Before Hilary could reply Rick had jumped in for her, saying casually, "The opportunity to work where she's really needed, what else?" He glanced at Hilary meaningfully, silently telling her that it was okay, he would handle this sticky questioning. "Unfortunately," he sighed, looking back over at Emma. "I couldn't talk her into staying on indefinitely." He winked at everyone in the room. "Although I admit I am still trying and will be for some time." Everyone laughed.

Hilary relaxed slightly, but to her continuing chagrin Emma looked more curious with every passing second.

Fortunately by then patients had started to arrive. Rick treated a man with an infected hand, another with a bad cough, a third with a sprained wrist. Hilary looked at a woman with recurring migraine headaches, a young man with a rash and an older man with bursitis, among others. By noon, she felt some of her old confidence, her old energy returning.

"I'm going to call over to the garage and see if your truck is finished yet," Rick said, a smile on his face indicating she'd done a good job.

She nodded, and began to pack her things up. Emma came back over to Hilary. "So, I guess your specialty is general medicine, too," she said.

"Uh, no," Hilary had to admit, feeling uncomfortable as the topic of conversation tread closer to the malpractice case lodged against her. She felt a blush of humiliation warm her cheeks. "It actually was obstetrics."

"Then you'll be delivering babies here, too?" Emma asked, looking momentarily delighted as the news of Hilary's specialty sank in.

"I'm afraid not," Rick said, coming back over to join them, saving Hilary the mixed pain and mortification of having to respond. "The county won't spring for the malpractice insurance for obstetrics for either of us, since we don't have a hospital to practice in. You ladies are still going to have to go into Lexington for Dr. Leiberman's help on that."

"But that's a seventy-five mile trip, one way!" Emma protested, perturbed.

"I know. But they also have a hospital there with a fully equipped maternity ward and facilities for preemies. Sorry, ladies." Rick turned to Hilary, his manner officious. Suddenly he seemed in a hurry to get out of there. "We have a lot to do today. We better get a move on."

Silence fell between them as they drove off. Hilary's thoughts went back to Emma. Because of what had happened to her in Boston, she knew she had to pursue what technically, anyway, might be none of her business. "Do you know Emma's obstetrician?"

Rick tore his eyes from the road long enough to send her a puzzled glance. "Yes, why?"

Hilary kept her eyes on the ruggedly beautiful countryside. "I couldn't help but notice as Emma asked me questions about my background that her wrists and ankles were swollen. She seems to be retaining water. I think she should be looked at. I didn't want to say anything because she's not my patient. Protocol, you know."

"Thanks for noticing," he said quietly, after a moment. "I'll call Dr. Leiberman and let him know. If

Emma can't get time off to drive into Lexington to see him, I'll see her over at the clinic and consult with him by phone." He gave her an assessing look and added slowly, "You're good, you know. That would've slipped right by me."

Hilary nodded. She just wished she had been that alert in Mrs. Jones's case.

Happily, when they got to the garage, Hilary's truck was all ready to go. To her delight, it was a four-wheel-drive pickup with a dark green exterior. About ten years newer than Rick's model, the interior seat had been covered with a soft beige fabric. She turned to Rick. "Did you have your choice of trucks?"

After a moment, he nodded.

"You gave me the better truck?"

He nodded again, shrugging it off as if it were no big deal. "I figured it was more important for you to have reliable transportation than me." He reached into his glove compartment and pulled out several large county maps. "I don't think it'll take you too long to learn your way around, but keep these with you, just in case."

"Thanks," she said, grateful and touched he had given so much thought to her comfort. It seemed he had thought of everything.

Grabbing a bite to eat, they drove on to the clinic. Housed in a frame building, it nestled among a cluster of businesses that composed the town of Crossings. The businesses included a gas station, a marketplace, a small postal station and a garage that housed a small fire truck and ambulance.

Inside the clinic, Hilary was just as depressed by the lack of facilities. "Three times a week I have a visiting nurse come in and help with the paperwork and whatever else needs to be done, but that's it—otherwise you're on your own. We run our own simple lab tests whenever possible—mostly because it's easier and cheaper than trying to send them out. We've got an X-ray machine in back, a crash cart and, of course, oxygen, but nothing else."

"Except our wits and our guts," Hilary said.

He met her eyes then gave her a small, easy grin that she gladly returned. "You seem to have plenty of both."

Hilary was still glowing from his unexpected praise when the door opened and their first patient of the day came in. "What do you say we alternate today?" Rick suggested. "You see a patient, then I'll see one."

Hilary smiled and nodded.

By the time the day ended, she was doubly tired as when she had started. Rick wanted her to stay with his mom, but she declined, confident the electricity was on, the wood pile well-stocked and the squirrels gone. Besides she wanted to be alone, so she could sort out the day's events.

Following the map he gave her, she drove the winding country roads to her new home. It amazed her to see the disparity in housing: A modern two-story colonial here, sat next to a broken-down trailer. An old home next to a tract home. Common features they all shared were satellite dishes or huge television antennae. She supposed that meant there was no cable out here. She heaved another sigh. Something else to get accustomed to living without.

By the time she drove up the shady lane, it was almost six-thirty. Another truck sat parked in her yard—one as old and beat-up as Rick's. A young man who couldn't have been more than eighteen was kneeling beside her front porch, hammering the last of some very solid-looking two-by-fours into place. He looked up when she alighted and walked toward him. Sweat was pouring from his brow.

He took a handkerchief from the back pocket of his cutoff jeans and wiped his face and hands. "Hi, you must be Doc Morgan. I'm Kenny Burnett, Rick's brother. He sent me over to fix this porch."

Kenny's hair was the same wheat-blond as Rick's, his eyes just as gray. And yet they were as different as night and day. For one thing, Kenny was incredibly shy and Hilary was willing to bet Rick didn't have a shy bone in his body. "Hi, Kenny," she said warmly, offering her hand. "It's nice to meet you." She stepped back to peer beneath the porch. She was pleased to see he had boarded it up tight as a drum. "Get all the squirrels out?"

"Yes, ma'am. All the nests, too. They had quite a few hickory nuts and walnuts stored under there, too.

I raked 'em all out and took their food over to the woods, so they could get at it.'' He pointed to the stand of trees that separated her place from the adjacent tobacco farm. "I don't think they'll be back to bother you."

"Thanks. I really appreciate it." She opened her handbag and reached for her billfold. "What do I owe you?"

Kenny held up his hands, to signal he couldn't take any money from her. "Rick's already said he'll pay me."

She owed Rick Burnett far too much, as it was. His family had fed her, helped her clean up, offered to put her up for the night, and now this, too. Hilary wasn't comfortable being too indebted to anyone. She preferred to hold her own. She smiled at Kenny. "I want to pay you. It's my house, I think I should."

But he raised his hand in a dismissive gesture and headed for his truck. "I've got to run. Daisy and I gotta drive into Lexington and pick out a tux for my wedding."

As he climbed into his truck, Hilary couldn't help but admire his strong back, which reminded her of Rick. A much younger Rick, albeit. She sighed wistfully, admiring the robustness of youth.

As she stepped inside, the phone began to ring. Picking it up, she was surprised and pleased to hear Rick's familiar voice on the other end of the line.

"Hilary? Rick. Everything okay there? Squirrels gone and the crawl space boarded up? Your electricity on?"

"Yes to all the above," Hilary said, amused at the rapid-fire way he was getting off questions and eliciting answers from her.

"Good. Listen, I'm having the county medical staff—all the visiting nurses and the four other doctors from the other two counties—over to my place for dinner. They'd all like to meet you. You interested?"

Hilary tensed. Since the lawsuit she'd been vaguely uncomfortable around other doctors, and that went triple for those she didn't know. On the other hand, she was curious about the others who worked there, and knew it would be to her benefit to meet them. "Sounds good to me," she said after a moment, forcing a genial note into her voice. Opening her purse, she scrounged for a ballpoint pen and paper. Juggling the receiver between her ear and her shoulder, she clicked the pen into writing position. "Just give me directions to your place."

He answered with a low laugh. "Forget it. You'd never find it in the dark, and I've got no desire to spend my evening driving around in search of you. I'll pick you up. Seven o'clock okay?"

Hilary glanced at her watch. That would give her a little less than half an hour. "Yes, but—"

"Fine, I'll see you then," he said briskly and hung up before she could ask him what to wear. Briefly, Hilary thought about calling him back, but then decided against it. She was thirty-one years old. She knew how to dress. It wasn't as if she hadn't been to staff dinner parties before.

She went to her suitcase and pulled out a blue silk dinner dress that brought out the blue of her eyes. She was just putting the last pin into her upswept black hair when she heard Rick's pickup in the drive.

She grabbed her evening purse and went to get the door. Rick was standing on the porch, in jeans and a white cotton shirt. He looked great, and she was overdressed. Way overdressed.

"I thought..." She bit down on her lip. Realizing how vastly different their expectations were, it was all she could do hide her embarrassment.

His glance roved over her slender form. "I guess I should have told you this was going to be an outdoor barbecue. You, uh, you might want to put on something a little less fancy." He shrugged, as if it didn't matter to him one way or another, and slid his hands in to his pockets. "Up to you."

If anything, his casual attitude toward her faux pas only heightened her embarrassment. Her cheeks burning, she lifted her chin and said, with as much cool as she could muster, "It won't take me long to change."

Minutes later, she emerged from her bedroom in a soft white cotton sweater, with blue flowers embroidered on the front, and a blue calico skirt.

"Sorry about that," Rick said, as his eyes drank her in appreciatively once again.

Hilary shook it off. This was country. She should have guessed that people here didn't have many occasions—except for church—to dress up. It was all she could do to suppress a sigh. It was clear her love of beautiful clothes would go to waste here, as would most of her wardrobe. To really fit in, she would have to dress as simply and inexpensively as everyone else. With that thought in mind, she followed Rick into the night.

"SO WHAT DO YOU THINK?" Rick asked as he parked in front of a spectacular log-cabin home. The two-story structure, with its rectangular design, had a wraparound front porch and plenty of picture windows. There were two stone chimneys, one at either end of the house.

"It's spectacular," she said, stunned almost beyond the point of speech. She had expected him to live in a place similar to hers. But then, maybe this house wasn't owned by the county. It was so nice! So...sophisticated, in an admittedly rustic way. "Is it yours?"

He nodded proudly. "I had it built when I moved here. Contractors put up the outside, but I did all the interior work and the finishing myself. Come on. I'll show you around before everyone else arrives."

Together, they walked up a flagstone path to the porch. A wooden swing hung at one end. Rough-hewn chairs made from unstripped tree limbs and lined with red cushions, decorated the porch.

Inside was just as rustic. A red-and-white U-shaped sofa sat in front of the massive stone hearth. The oak coffee table was a refinished antique. The rough-hewn plank floors matched the light golden hue of the cabin walls. A long staircase led to a loft upstairs. "The interior is beautiful, Rick. You obviously know your way around a hardware store."

He grinned, flattered. "Maybe I could help you fix up your place, too. You know, hang wallpaper, or whatever it is you want to do."

"Thanks, but I don't know how much more work I'm going to put into it. Since I'm not going to be here all that long... it may be pointless."

Rick's face remained expressionless. "You think the lawsuit will be settled soon?"

"I don't know," she said quietly. And even if it was, she didn't know if she would ever be able to go back to obstetrics. But she also knew, whatever happened, that she would eventually go back to the city.

Aware Rick still hadn't spoken, she studied his face. "That bothers you, doesn't it?" she said quietly after a moment. "The fact I'm only going to be here a short time."

He shrugged noncommittally, then looked her squarely in the eyes. "I admit I don't want anyone with a short-timer's attitude on my staff."

His bluntness robbed her of speech momentarily. "Do you think I have that?"

He raised and lowered his shoulders noncommittally. "In light of what you just said, are you telling me you don't?"

He was right, she did have a short-timer's attitude. She saw his point, that this wasn't necessarily good, even if it was realistic. Silence fell between them, lingered. Hilary looked down at her feet, then back up at his face. She had to be honest with him, they owed one another that. "You know the only reason I'm here is because I'm being sued."

He nodded slowly, not looking any happier.

"I'll do my best while I'm here, Rick. I'll give it my all," she promised, meaning every word.

The doubt in his eyes faded slowly. "Good."

As the tension between them lessened, she breathed a sigh of relief, glad they'd declared a truce, then instantly began to worry again. Maybe this wasn't going to be as easy as she'd thought. Especially if others viewed her temporariness there as undesirable, too.

Fortunately they were saved from further discussion when other staff members arrived. While Rick lit the grill out back, she met the other doctors and nurses. All were from that part of Kentucky, and could have left for higher paying city jobs after acquiring their education but had instead elected to return to practice in the impoverished part of the state where they had grown up. Listening to them talk, she felt even more of an outsider.

"So...do you have a house in Boston?" Will Parker asked casually, as they seated themselves at the pine table. A pediatrician in his late forties, he had returned to eastern Kentucky after completing his residency in a Lexington hospital, and had been there ever since. His wife Becca was the center's part-time nurse.

"No, just an apartment," she replied. She hadn't saved enough to manage a down payment on a condo, although she had eventually planned to do just that.

Will looked pleased she hadn't put down more permanent roots in Boston. She avoided thinking about what that might mean—that the people might be planning to pressure her to stay on because she was needed so badly.

"You know, I used to be a city girl," Becca said, helping herself to a hamburger from the platter that was making the rounds. "Grew up in Louisville. Never thought I'd be happy out here in the sticks. But I am, and so are our three kids."

Hilary smiled and nodded, but said nothing to indicate she was thinking about doing the same. She wouldn't encourage Will or Becca or anyone else there to think she might be persuaded to stay on in Kentucky, no matter how charming or gregarious or helpful they all were. As varied and challenging an interlude as this was proving to be for her, it was still just that—a temporary solution.

The rest of dinner passed swiftly, with Rick and the other doctors swapping stories about their med-school days. Soon they were all laughing. And it was only when she and Rick were en route home again, several hours later, that they had a chance to talk to one another.

"By the way," he said, as he parked in front of her house and cut the motor, "I have a patient I'd like you to see tomorrow. Mrs. Orlansky. She lives on Pine Mountain. She's a tough old bird, about seventy-five, as near as I can tell. You might have better luck with her than I have."

"What's wrong with her?" Hilary asked, getting out and circling around the truck to walk with Rick up to her front porch.

"I'm not sure." Rick leaned a shoulder against the door frame, watching as she slid the key into the lock. "She's always been someone who's pretty much kept to herself. One of her neighbors noticed she's lost a lot of weight and has been looking real bad. The neighbor called me to see if someone would come out. I went, but she wouldn't let me in. Same with the public-health nurse. Clara's, uh...kind of superstitious and crotchety, and her ill health has made her even more irritable. Anyway, she doesn't hold much with doctors or medical people of any kind, and she's bound and determined not to leave Pine Mountain or that broken-down house of hers. I thought you might have better luck with her. At any rate it's worth a try."

Hilary bit her lower lip worriedly; what he was describing sounded far from easy. How could she, a virtual stranger, hope to inspire faith and treat this woman? Yet that was exactly what he was asking her to do.

"Write down the address for me, and directions on how to get there. I'll see what I can do," she promised after a moment. Considering all he'd done for her, she was delighted to be able to return the favor. She only hoped she was up to the task, and that he was right to put his faith in her. She didn't want to fail a patient, not ever again.

Chapter Three

I might as well face it. I'm lost, Hilary thought as she slowed the noisy old pickup truck to a halt near the side of the road. Getting the map from the glove compartment, she began trying to figure out where she was—to no avail. None of the side roads was very well marked, and she had a growing suspicion that teenagers had turned some of the signs around, because the route she thought she had traveled had not resembled the route she had marked out on the map.

Sighing, she put the truck in gear and started on up the road. She would get out and ask directions at the first house she saw. It was either that or be lost forever.

The next home she confronted was situated in a "hollar"—as she had learned the valleys between the hills were called in Kentucky—about a half mile up the road. The faded yellow double-width trailer was sitting up on cement blocks. Garbage was strewn out over the yard. There was no car in sight, but a little girl of about eight was playing in the yard. Barefoot and filthy from head to toe, she twirled a baton round and round, tossing it up in the air and catching it. Hilary smiled as she watched the little girl agilely jump up and make a very difficult catch.

The little girl whirled in surprise when Hilary pulled her truck into the gravel drive and parked it. She looked even more wary when, map in hand, Hilary got out. "Hello!" she called cheerfully. "I'm Dr. Morgan. Is your mom or dad home? I'm afraid I'm lost and I need to ask someone directions."

The little girl looked up, her mouth a round "O" of surprise, fear in her light brown eyes. Without a word, she ran and slammed the door of the trailer shut, her long dirty blond hair flying out behind her. The lock clicked seconds later.

Hilary waited, figuring an adult would come out any minute. But as the seconds ticked by and no one appeared, she began to suspect no one else was home. The thought disturbed her because the frail-looking little girl was really too small to be left by herself, especially so far out in the country away from obvious help. Worse, she knew she had frightened the girl badly. She didn't want to leave without comforting her.

She went to the door of the trailer and knocked. When there was no response she knocked again, loudly. "Honey, I'm sorry if I frightened you. I'm leaving now. You don't need to worry. I won't hurt you.''

A portion of the dingy curtain was pulled aside. The little girl peered out, a frown creasing her pinched little mouth. "Are you really a doctor?" she said.

Hilary nodded and gave her a reassuring smile. "I sure am. I work with Dr. Burnett. Do you know Rick?"

After a moment, the little girl nodded. She smiled tremulously as she admitted, "He gives me lollipops."

Hilary smiled. "Well, I'm going to work in the same clinic with Dr. Burnett." She held up a piece of paper with her name and phone number, plus the reason she'd stopped by, then placed it on the cement step in front of the door. "When your mom or dad comes back give them this note and tell them I was here, okay?" She didn't want anyone worried needlessly about some "stranger" prowling the countryside.

After a moment, the little girl nodded.

Hilary was about to leave when she decided to try one more thing. "What's your name?" she asked.

"Clem," the little girl said shyly. "Clementine Morris."

Clementine stayed on Hilary's mind long after she left, as she continued to find her way to her elderly patient's house.

There she received no warmer welcome than she had from Clementine Morris. The old lady hobbled out on her porch and aimed a walking stick at Hilary before she took more than a step up the crookedly laid front walk. She was dressed in a faded housedress and slippers, with a calico apron tied over that. "Hold it right there, young woman," Mrs. Orlansky said. "I ain't buying nothing."

If the woman hadn't been so obviously frail and arthritic, Hilary would have found the threat comical. Hilary forced another smile. "I'm not selling anything. I'm Dr. Morgan." She held out her hand in greeting, but the friendly gesture was ignored. With a sigh, she dropped her hand to her side. "Dr. Burnett asked me to look in on you."

Mrs. Orlansky snorted impatiently and waved her away. "I don't need no lookin' in on."

Hilary disagreed. It was clear the seventy-five-year-old woman was in very poor health. She was so weak she could hardly stand, despite her efforts to appear formidable. "I'm not going to charge you anything, Mrs. Orlansky. My services are paid for by the county."

"I don't care who paid. Don't come any closer!" Mrs. Orlansky said, waving her stick threateningly again.

Hilary sighed. She was not going to get anywhere with Mrs. Orlansky this morning. She would just have to come back and try later. "All right, Mrs. Orlansky. I have no interest in examining a patient who doesn't want to be seen," she said finally. "But I wonder if I might trouble you for a glass of water. The morning's getting awfully warm and I haven't had a drink." Maybe if she could just befriend her a little, she'd eventually get the woman to trust her. It wouldn't hurt to try, anyway.

The older woman looked at the sweat beading Hilary's brow. Then she shook her head, and turned to go back in the house. "There's a grocery store five miles down the road, at the bottom of Pine Mountain. You can get you a drink of water there." The door slammed behind her.

And that, it seemed, was that.

So much for Kentucky hospitality, Hilary thought, going back to the truck. Unfortunately the rest of her morning did not go much smoother. She got lost twice en route back to the clinic in Crossings, and was almost out of gas by the time her truck made it into town.

As she got out of her truck, Rick pulled up beside her. In contrast to her slightly disheveled state, he looked cool and energetic. "So how'd your morning go?" he asked, getting out of his truck, a sheaf of folders in one hand, his medical bag in the other.

Hilary slammed her door shut. "It didn't," she reported baldly. Briefly, she told him about her morning.

"Well, I can't say as I'm surprised. Mrs. Orlansky was never the friendly type to begin with, and since her husband of fifty-five years died last year, she's become even more reclusive."

"Does she have any relatives?" Hilary asked, searching for a way around the problem. "Any children we might go to for help?"

He shook his head sadly. "No, Clara Orlansky never had any children. And whatever relatives she had have either died or moved away. She's a real loner, that one."

"So what are we going to do?" Carrying her bag in her hand, Hilary followed Rick into the small, sparsely furnished clinic.

"There's not much we can do at the moment. She doesn't seem to be in any immediate physical danger, although she has lost a lot of weight lately." He frowned. "How was she, otherwise?"

"Cranky, weak, maybe a little arthritic."

Rick sighed and ran both hands through his wheat-blond hair. "I had hoped—you being a woman, and all—that you might have more success with her, but I guess I was wrong. Sorry to have put you through that." He picked up the mail and began sorting through it.

Remembering Clementine Morris, Hilary told Rick about that, too. He frowned, when she said that the little girl had apparently been alone. "Her mom died a couple of years ago and her dad works over at the coal mine. He's a foreman there, but her cousin Daisy is supposed to be keeping an eye on Clem during the summer." He swore again.

"Daisy," Hilary repeated, trying to think where she'd heard that name. "Is that—?"

"Kenny's girlfriend. One and the same." Rick tossed the mail down. "I'll have a talk with Wilbur about this." He picked up the phone and dialed the mine. About thirty minutes later, he explained.

"Clementine wasn't alone. Daisy was there. She was doing some sewing in the back bedroom while she listened to music, and apparently she didn't hear your truck drive up."

Hilary stared at him, astonished. "What kind of baby-sitter is that?"

Rick shrugged and answered on a sigh. "She's still a child herself, a teenager. Anyway, Wilbur set her straight. They've agreed she needs to keep a closer eye on Clem."

"Good!" Hilary expressed her relief. But that still didn't explain why the little girl had looked so unkempt and dirty. Being poor didn't have to mean being dirty. Hilary couldn't help but think that Clementine needed an extra dose of tender, loving care—that her father might have been too preoccupied or pressured to give. She determined to keep an eye out for the little girl in the future.

"LOOK, YOU'RE REAL PRETTY and all," the young man in overalls said Friday afternoon as blood trickled from a bandaged gash on his forearm, "but I want a real doctor. Like Rick. Somebody who knows how to fix us country folks up. Not some city slicker fresh out of medical school…who's only here cause…well, heck, I don't know why you're here, but…I want Rick working on me. Nobody else."

Hilary gave the young man her most reassuring smile. "I promise you I've had plenty of training in emergency suturing." She started toward him.

He drew back his arm, refusing to let her so much as touch him. "That's real nice," he said, glaring at her suspiciously, "but you ain't trying out any of that training on me. I ain't no guinea pig. I want Rick."

Hilary could see she hadn't a chance of persuading him otherwise. "Have a seat," she said as graciously as she could, working to suppress her disappointment. This same type of reaction had happened over and over all week. Why was she here if she couldn't help? "I'll get him."

Fortunately Rick was almost done with the patient he was seeing. "Cheer up, it'll get better once people here get to know you," he said, as he went to retrieve the patient in need of suturing.

Hilary wondered if that was true. It seemed to her that no one there trusted outsiders, and to many of them she was a young, single, city slicker who had no more place here than they had in the city.

Returning to her office, Hilary picked up the latest copy of the *New England Journal of Medicine*. If she couldn't see patients, she could at least read up on the latest developments in medicine. One way or another, she was determined to get something positive out of her stay in Kentucky. For the next hour she immersed herself in the latest treatment for Alzheimer's, meningococcal meningitis, and gastroschisis. Now that she was practicing general medicine again, she needed to be versed in a variety of illnesses.

"Hilary, can you come in here?" Rick called from his examining room an hour later.

Anxious to be of help, Hilary abandoned the medical journal she had been reading and raced across the hall. Emma Schwartz was sitting on the examining table, wearing a dressing gown that buttoned up the back. Remembering the Environmental Protection Agency official from the coal-mine office, Hilary gave her a brief smile she couldn't begin to feel. At that moment she didn't think she could take one more query on why she had given up obstetrics and Boston to practice general medicine in the little town of Crossings, Kentucky.

"Emma's been retaining water. So far her blood pressure is fine and she doesn't have any history of—"

As Rick began filling her in on the details of Emma's pregnancy, Hilary felt the first stirrings of panic and uneasiness. He knew better than to consult with her on any obstetrics case. Right now, the way she was feeling, she couldn't deal with it. "I'm sorry,

Emma," Hilary interrupted before Rick could tell her more. "Rick, may I speak to you a moment alone?"

He glanced back at Emma, who was looking a little bewildered. He shrugged and said, "Sure." Then, to Emma, "Be right back."

"Okay, doc," Emma said cheerfully, a curious look on her face.

Rick closed the door behind him. "I thought she was going to see Dr. Leiberman in Lexington," Hilary began, trying to quell the unaccustomed fear and anxiety she felt welling up inside her. This case had no similarity at all to the Jones case. What happened there, wouldn't happen again...

"He's on vacation for two weeks, as it turns out. Emma asked me to handle it until he gets back, and considering the distance she was going to have to drive and the fact she doesn't seem to be in any emergency situation, I agreed to examine her. I thought I could see what I could do to slow down or eliminate her water retention."

Hilary was not appeased by his explanation. Her face was flushed with the humiliation she felt at having been put in an awkward situation, not to mention the legal ramifications. "You know I can't consult with you, Rick," Hilary said wearily.

"Not formally, no, but—"

"Not informally, either," she continued with soft finality. If something did go wrong, if they got sued, it would ruin not just Hilary's career but probably

Rick's career, as well. The clinic would probably also be held financially liable. Knowing how badly the county facility was needed to serve patients in the impoverished area, it wasn't a risk Hilary thought they ought to take.

Wordlessly Rick ushered her into the tiny private office where he did his paperwork and made his telephone calls to patients. "Hilary, I understand your reluctance, but this isn't a big-city hospital where there are dozens of doctors to consult with. If I need you, you have to remember our circumstances here. It's as simple as that."

Hilary intended to help where and when she could, but right now he was asking too much, especially when there was a much better, safer route to take. "Call whoever is covering for Leiberman in Lexington. Ask them to see her or discuss the specifics of her case with you."

Rick stared at her, perplexed. He knew she was competent to handle this, but obviously she didn't. He hadn't realized—although maybe he should have—that the lawsuit had unnerved her so. Wanting to reassure her, he lowered his voice persuasively, "You have extensive training in OB, Hilary. All I'm asking is for you to share some of that knowledge with me, to help me care for Emma." He paused, letting his words sink in, then added his worst fear. "She's showing some early signs of mild pre-eclampsia. I need a diagnosis."

Hilary bit her lip in consternation as the information she had learned over the years rushed back to her. Pre-eclampsia was a disorder of late pregnancy, where a mother's blood pressure rises and her body retains excess fluids. The condition could be very dangerous, especially late in pregnancy. It required constant monitoring and careful handling—none of which she could currently give, both of which Emma needed. Fortunately Emma was still in her fifth month, the situation not so far out-of-hand yet that anything drastic, such as hospitalizing the mother, was needed.

Nonetheless, as much as she wanted to help him, she couldn't. The circumstances of her personal situation forbade it. She looked at him, not bothering to mask her regret. "The answer is still no, Rick."

He made no effort to cover his disappointment. "You won't help at all—even temporarily?" His tone wasn't an indictment, rather a simple statement of fact.

He seemed to sense it wasn't just her lack of insurance stopping her, but he also knew she wasn't willing to discuss it further.

Without condemnation, Rick turned and went back to his patient. Soon she heard him on the phone to Lexington. Calmly she removed the stethoscope she had wrapped around her neck, and took off her white lab coat. Aware her legs were shaking, and that she needed to get away, she left the office and drove home.

Once back at her house, she was restless, irritable. Feeling she had to do something or go crazy, she dragged the scarred coffee table out onto the front lawn and began sanding it down. She was just applying the first coat of varnish she'd bought earlier in the week when Rick's truck pulled into the lane.

Not wanting to acknowledge the way her heart had started pounding at the sight of him, she continued with her work, refusing to look up when he finally stood next to her short moments later.

He sank down beside her, resting one elbow on his knee. She expected him to apologize for asking her to do the impossible. Instead he observed softly, "You really got burned back in Boston, didn't you?"

Without warning, there was a lump in her throat the size of a walnut and moisture burning her eyes. Embarrassed and humiliated to be so near tears, she refused to look at him. She never cried. She wouldn't start now. She could handle this. She just had to take a deep breath. "I wouldn't describe it that way," she said finally.

He sat down on the grass beside her, folding his legs beneath him Indian-style. "Tell me about it."

She knew he already had all the details—they'd been given to him at the time she applied for the county job. But he didn't know how she felt about it. No one did, because she never talked about it. Deciding finally it might be cathartic, she told him, starting with Mrs. Jones's first visit to her and ending with the day she lost the baby. "The hardest part for me is knowing that if the timing of her office visit and miscarriage had been just a little bit different—if I'd seen her twenty-four hours prior to the miscarriage—that there might have been some sign. I might have been able to act in time to save her baby."

"Maybe not," Rick differed gently. Her head lifted and he continued with quiet conviction, "If I remember correctly, that particular condition isn't evident until after the fourteenth week of pregnancy. There's typically very little warning. So in all probability there was nothing for you to pick up on during Mrs. Jones's last exam, particularly if she wasn't having any symptoms."

Was he right? Was she free of blame in this? Hilary wished she could think so, too, but right now she just wasn't sure. And she wasn't certain she ever would be. Silence fell between them as she finished varnishing and then began to clean up. Rick was quiet, thinking, gauging her mood.

Aware he was shadowing her, but not minding his presence now that the tension between them had eased, she walked to the lean-to shed on the side of the house and put the varnish can on the shelf. She put the brush into a jar of soapy water to soak. He waited just inside the door, his shoulder braced against the door frame, his arms crossed over his chest. She was aware suddenly of how small the interior was, how close they were physically—and on another level, as well.

It took every bit of strength she had to brace herself and move past him, out into the open again. He followed her out into the yard, his long, lazy steps eating up twice the distance of hers.

"About what happened today," she said firmly, pausing in the middle of the yard. "I'm not changing my mind about consulting with you about Emma Schwartz or any other pregnant woman." It was important to her that Rick understand that; she didn't want them having this discussion again. It opened up too many wounds and brought forth too many of her insecurities.

He kept his eyes on hers. "You don't have to. I've already asked another doctor in Lexington to consult." She breathed a sigh of relief and he went on smoothly, his conviction steadfast. "But we have to face facts here, Hilary," he said reasonably. "We're an hour or more from a hospital. There are a number of pregnant women in the area. There may come a time when we have an emergency and you're the closest we've got to an obstetrician around here—"

"No." Hilary backed away from him, furious now, that after all she'd told him, after the way she'd poured out her heart, that he would still expect her to advise on pregnancy cases.

He sighed. He trusted her as a physician, and knew the people here needed her expertise. He knew medical malpractice cases were not always a doctor's fault. Most of all, deeper issues were involved, personal ones to Hilary. "You'll never get your confidence back if you don't get back into obstetrics, at least peripherally."

She warmed to his understanding, but stood firm. "I mean it, Rick. This is a position I have to take if I stay here."

He ran impatient fingers through his hair and swore beneath his breath. "If that's really the way you feel, fine. I'll respect your position. I won't press you again," he moved toward her and squeezed a shoulder tenderly. Then he turned and went to the door. "See you tomorrow?"

She nodded, amazed by his warmth, his understanding. When he left quietly, she was also amazed how bereft she felt.

Chapter Four

Emma Schwartz pushed her way in the following morning, shortly after Hilary had opened up the clinic.

"I want you to know I know all about your Boston fiasco," Emma said, fixing her with a stony glare that conjured up all of Hilary's guilt. "My cousin goes to the doctor in the next county over and she overheard him talking about it, so don't try and deny it. For the good of the public, you have no choice but to resign from your job with county health."

Seconds later, Rick walked in. Hearing the tail end of what was going on, his face got very red and there was a distinct warning in his silver eyes. "Emma, you're out of line here."

"Says who?"

Rick looked at Emma with narrowed eyes, ignoring the emotion vibrating in her voice. "Says our justice system. A person is innocent until proven guilty."

Emma glanced uncertainly around the room. "I'm not having my baby delivered by someone with a law-suit hanging over them."

"You won't have to; Dr. Leiberman is going to de-liver your baby, remember? Hilary is only here to practice general medicine, which she is very well qual-ified to do. Now go—patients are arriving."

Emma paused a moment. Without a word, she whirled and strode out. Rick looked at Hilary. "You okay?"

She didn't feel okay. There was a sick feeling in the pit of her stomach and her knees were so weak she could barely stand, nonetheless pride forced her to say, "I'm fine." Turning, she headed for her private of-fice near the back of the clinic, her sneakers moving soundlessly on the scrubbed linoleum floor. He fol-lowed her into the tiny cubicle and shut the door softly behind them.

Aware of the perspiration beading her face, she sat down behind her desk.

He seated himself on the corner of her desk. "She'll cool down. Once you have a chance to do some good in the community, people will see what kind of doctor you are. They'd resist any newcomer, you know."

Hilary was silent. He was taking a lot for granted. After all, she'd seen the looks on those people's faces. They were scared. And maybe, considering what had happened to the Jones baby, they should be. Maybe...as much as she wanted to be a healer...she wasn't cut out for this. "Maybe I should quit," she said quietly, aware her eyes were suddenly burning with unshed tears.

She'd had enough of being where she wasn't wanted when she was still in Boston.

Rick gave her an affectionate look that urged her not to surrender. "You can't quit. You've got a contract with the county, remember?"

Hilary remembered, all too well. And she was more anxious than ever to be back on familiar turf, to work in an area where she could do some good. Evidently, for a variety of reasons, that wasn't here. "My contract can be broken." Her lawyer, Dash Barrington, had made sure of that before she signed it. "Rick—"

He held up a hand, stopping the onslaught of words on the tip of her tongue. "Give it time, Hilary. People will come around."

He seemed so sure of himself. She wished she had just a smidgeon of his confidence, his strength of purpose. Obliquely, she wondered if he would have the same solid, sensible, practical approach to love as he did to work. And she wondered why it should matter to her.

"Well?" Rick said patiently. "Are you willing to wait it out or not?"

Like it or not, Hilary had plenty of time. She'd never liked leaving anything to chance, but in this case what other choice did she have? Besides, where else was she going to go? Until resolved, the court case would follow her. She stood restlessly. "How can you be so sure of me, Rick?" Although she'd seen his doubts about her reflected from time to time in his eyes, there had been none of that when he'd spoken in the waiting room.

"Because I feel it in here." He thumped his chest. "You're okay. You care about patients. You take the time with them that they need. And you don't hesitate to back off when you feel you're out of your league."

His praise warmed her heart, but she still felt like a stranger in a strange land. *Give it time*, he'd said.

"I'll try," she said finally, acknowledging the truth behind his words.

He smiled encouragingly. "That's the way."

Unfortunately news spread fast in Crossings, and few if any patients were willing to see her. They all preferred to wait for Rick. Hilary allowed herself to feel hurt for about an hour, then decided enough of that. She'd come there to do some good, and that was precisely what she was going to do.

Taking off her lab coat, she reached for her medical bag. She stopped by Rick's office while he was between patients, to tell him where she was going. "I'm going to drive out to Pine Mountain and have another go round with Mrs. Orlansky."

He smiled. "That's the spirit."

She only hoped her impromptu plan would work.

This time, she didn't get lost once on the drive out. Feeling rather proud of herself for having successfully navigated the tricky roads, she parked at the end of the drive.

As before, Clara Orlansky was out on her porch almost the moment Hilary set foot from the truck. She waved her walking stick at Hilary. "I told you before, young woman. I don't want no help!"

Hilary marched forward, her medical bag clutched tightly in her hand, her chin high. "That's too bad, Mrs. Orlansky because you're going to get some help if I have to drag the local sheriff out here to do it!"

Clara's jaw dropped. She stared at Hilary. "You can't do that," she asserted disbelievingly, after a moment.

Hilary kept right on closing the distance between them. "The hell I can't. You just watch and see." She advanced up the steps, not breaking stride once. "Now what's it going to be, Clara?"

"You ain't got no right to be calling me by my given name."

"I suppose not. Mrs. Orlansky, then."

The old woman peered at her suspiciously. "There ain't nothing you can give me that's going to make me feel any better, you know. I'm an old woman. I'm gonna die soon."

Not if Hilary could help it.

She walked past Mrs. Orlansky and opened the screen door. "Shall we go in here?"

FIFTEEN MINUTES LATER, the cursory examination was complete. Clara's heart was sound, as were her lungs, but she had a swollen thyroid gland that Hilary suspected was symptomatic of a much more serious problem. "I need to run some blood tests on you," Hilary said.

"Oh, no," Clara said, buttoning up her faded housedress. It was much larger than her slender frame would have required. "You ain't taking none of my blood."

Hilary knew she was. But first, she needed more information. "Have you lost a lot of weight lately? Been very thirsty?" Clara nodded yes to both questions. "How's your appetite?" Hilary asked.

"Big as a mountain," Clara said. "I can't seem to get enough to eat these days. In fact, that's all I seem to do these days, cook and eat, cook and eat."

It all fit. But first, she needed blood work to confirm her suspicions. Only then would she be able to work up a treatment plan. One Clara would agree to follow.

"Would you like to feel better?" Hilary asked gently. "More like your old self? Not as tired?"

Clara's eyes lit up. "What you got in mind?"

"More tests."

"No—"

"I'll take your blood before I leave. Then I'll pack it in ice and run it into a hospital in Lexington myself, to see what they can discover. We won't get the results for a couple of days, but that can't be helped. It's important, Clara, otherwise I wouldn't ask." The old woman said nothing. "Please."

More silence. "You really think you can make me feel better?"

Hilary nodded, pleased she was getting somewhere. "If you've got what I think you have, I can guarantee it."

Clara shook her head and mumbled several sentences Hilary was just as glad she was unable to make out. She stared at Hilary distrustfully. "I ain't gonna get rid of you until I go along with you, am I?"

"Probably not."

Clara blew out a weary breath. "Well, make it quick," she said finally, rolling up her sleeve. "I ain't got all day."

"HYPERTHYROIDISM and insulin-dependent diabetes," Rick said, scanning the results of the lab tests early Tuesday morning. He looked over at Hilary, and favored her with a warm smile.

It was all Hilary could do not to blush.

"I'm impressed," Rick continued, still watching her in that peculiarly warm assessing way, that made her feel he was seeing her not just as a doctor or a friend, but as a woman too. A woman he'd like to get to know better.

Hilary worked to keep her voice level. "About what?"

"I'm impressed that you were able to come up with a diagnosis so quickly, and an accurate one at that." He peered at her closely, his thoughts returning to medical matters. "Maybe you missed your calling. Maybe you should have been a general practitioner."

She wondered if that was his roundabout way of saying that he thought she made a lousy obstetrician. Sighing, Hilary decided she was being silly. Right now their task was Mrs. Orlansky and what they could do for her.

"Thanks for the compliment," Hilary said, as she took back the file. "The question is, what do we do now?" She bit her lip and looked up at Rick. "You know as well as I, that getting Mrs. Orlansky treated is going to be ten times harder than getting her to submit to an initial exam and a couple of simple tests."

He held up both hands in a gesture of surrender. "Don't ask me. I never got this far with her."

Hilary looked at him drolly. Damn the man, anyway, she'd been counting on him for help in dealing with the locals and their mind-sets. So why did he have to back off now? "I know there's a reason I like you. Right now I can't remember what it is."

"Oh, I think you'll remember the next time the squirrels look for a new home." His eyes glimmered with amusement, making her fidget, before he continued earnestly, "But I'm serious about Clara, Hil— she's all yours. Just follow your instincts. They were good before. I'm sure they'll work again."

She studied him, impressed by his earnestness. Maybe Rick was right. Maybe she just needed to follow her instincts on this one. And just not let Mrs. Orlansky get out of doing the right thing. If that meant talking to her until she was blue in the face, then that's what she would do.

Getting back into her truck, she drove out to Clara's place. Mrs. Orlansky was sitting on the front porch. Spying Hilary, she waved her walking stick in her direction. "If you're here to stick me again, you can just forget it. You ain't getting any more of my blood."

Hilary strode up the path, determined not to let any of her inner trepidation show. She was in control here; she simply had to make Clara believe it, and believe in her and her vast stores of medical knowledge. Sitting down across from Clara, she launched into an immediate, detailed explanation of what was ailing the older woman, taking pains to explain the complicated blood chemistry in plain language. She finished, "What all this boils down to is that you're going to have to take a lot of medicine for a while."

Clara was silent, suspicious. "What happens if I don't take it?"

Hilary sensed she didn't want her to beat around the bush, but rather speak bluntly. "You'll die—a lot sooner than you need to."

"You trying to scare me?"

Hilary smiled faintly, aware that under the cantankerous bravura there was a very nice woman. "Yes. Is it working?"

Clara laughed abruptly and shook her head, trying hard not to show how shaken she was by what Hilary had just told her. "I ain't never seen anybody as bent on having their own way as you, missy."

Hilary took the compliment in the generous spirit it was given. "Yeah, and you probably won't, either. At least not around these parts." Giving her patient no more chance to argue, she said, "Now listen up. We have a lot to go over...."

"SO I'M TO STOP out there every other day," Becca Parker said several hours later.

"Until we know for certain that Mrs. Orlansky has gotten the hang of taking her insulin. She's still a little leery of needles, in general, and the idea of giving herself insulin is well, scary, to say the least."

Becca nodded. "You've done a good job with her. Rick is really impressed."

Hilary glanced up. "If only Clara Orlansky thought so."

Becca laughed. "You'd be surprised. You're already gaining some fans around town." She rose.

"Listen, I've gotta go. The natives may get restless. Keep your chin up."

Hilary waved at her as the nurse walked out of the room, closing the door behind her.

She had just put the finishing touches on a letter of resignation when the phone rang. She got up to get it. "Dr. Morgan."

"Oh, doctor, I'm so glad I got you. Something terrible's happened! Li'l Clementine has cut her foot. I don't have a car. She's in bad shape and I don't know what to do—"

In the background were prodigious wails and sobs. Daisy was obviously on the other line.

"Daisy—where are you? At the Morris's trailer?"

"Yes, please hurry, doctor! Please!"

Hilary got there as fast as she could. When she arrived ten minutes later, Clementine was still sobbing as if her heart would break. "Where's her father?" Hilary asked, setting her bag up on the table.

"Down in the mine. There's no way to get hold of him until his shift ends at six. Is she going to be all right?"

"I'll know better when I examine her."

Hilary lifted the weeping Clementine onto the kitchen counter, turning her so the injured foot was over the sink. Talking soothingly to her all the while, Hilary unwrapped the bloody towel from Clementine's foot. The cut was nasty and jagged, all right. At least an inch deep, it went from the arch clear to the ball of the foot. Seeing the wound, Clementine sobbed even more. Tears in her eyes, Daisy rushed over to hold her cousin.

The stitching took the better part of an hour. Clementine had stopped crying after Hilary injected her with a local anesthetic, but it was clear both girls were very, very shaken by what had happened. Had Daisy not been there to give aid and put pressure on the wound, Clem could easily have bled to death.

"What did this, anyway?" Hilary asked.

"I stepped on part of an old tin can."

Great, Hilary thought. She risked tetanus, too. "Was it rusty?"

Clementine and Daisy both nodded. Daisy asked, "Does that mean she's going to have to have a tetanus shot?"

Hilary nodded affirmatively. But to her surprise, Clementine didn't argue about it. In fact, looking at her face, the little girl looked absolutely exhausted.

"Daisy—" Hilary turned to the eighteen-year-old just in time to see her face turn the color of parchment. The next thing she knew Daisy had fainted.

DAISY MOANED. "I feel terrible."

The trauma of the accident had been a terrible strain on both girls. "Just stay down," Hilary counseled. In the back of the trailer, she had one girl on each of the twin beds. Since receiving the emergency call two hours before she hadn't stopped once, and it oc-

curred to Hilary how good it felt to be needed again.
She hadn't felt so useful in ages.

"You're nice," Clementine said sleepily, around a
yawn.

Hilary glanced down at the tired eight-year-old.
Although her injured leg had been washed clean to the
knee, the rest of her was in dire need of a bath. Her
hair was snarled and unkempt-looking, as were her
clothes. Yet Daisy was very well-groomed. Hilary felt
her anger build. Someone should be taking better care
of that little girl.

At that moment, the trailer door opened. A large
man in grubby coveralls walked in. "Daisy," he bel-
lowed back, "who does that truck out front belong
to?"

He stopped when he saw Hilary coming toward him.
His glance fell to the medical bag on the table.

"Hello, I'm Dr. Hilary Morgan. Your daughter had
an accident." While his face whitened, Hilary explained what had happened.

Wilbur Morris looked at first worried, then relieved. "But you stitched her up and everything? She's
okay?"

Hilary nodded. Although she knew it wasn't her
place to say so, she would hate to see this happen
again. Risky or not, she couldn't just stand by and say
nothing. "May I speak to you outside a moment,
please?"

Looking bewildered, he followed her out. "Mr. Morris, I think it would be better if you encouraged Clem to wear shoes on her feet at all times when she is outside."

"What are you talking about? It's summer. Kids always go barefoot in summer."

Out here they did, Hilary knew. That didn't change the fact it was a dangerous practice. "Mr. Morris, your yard is full of—" trash, Hilary was about to say, but decided diplomacy was the better part of valor "—potentially dangerous items. Rusty nails and cans that are half buried in the dirt, like the one Clem cut her foot on today. Pieces of broken glass. Mr. Morris, this could have been a lot worse—"

He thrust his thumbs into his belt and rolled back on his heels, scowling. "But it wasn't."

She could see she had offended him.

His jaw got even tighter. "Look, doc, I'm glad you stitched my little girl up, but don't think you can come around here telling me or my daughter how to live, because you can't." His eyes narrowed unpleasantly. "We don't need your interference."

And on that note, he slammed into the trailer without a backward glance.

So much for doing some good, Hilary thought.

Chapter Five

"You know, stitching up Clementine Morris's foot is one thing. Trying to tell Wilbur how to live is something else," Rick said, the moment she got back to the clinic.

Hilary went into her cubbyhole of an office and began writing up the report on Clementine's accident to add to her patient's file. Her motions were brisk and impatient, mirroring her mood.

"Have you seen his yard?" Finished, she snapped the cap on her pen and got up to file her report.

He spoke in a low, reasonable voice. "It's no worse than anyone else's."

"Maybe that's part of the problem," she said, slamming the file drawer with a decisive thud. "Being poor doesn't mean you have to live in filth, surrounded by trash."

He lifted a discerning brow. "I agree."

"I know. I've seen your house and your mother's." Both were well-kept in the extreme. "But there are tons of places around here that aren't clean. In fact, the yards are pigsties, filled with garbage—" She shuddered, thinking of the plentiful bacteria harbored in such germ-loving debris. It made her furious to see them neglected so.

"And you're the one to do it?" Despite her idealism, which was directly at war with his pragmatic nature, his voice was gentle, respectful. He seemed perplexed by her attitude, exasperated, rather than angered.

Hilary nodded, aware they were standing very close, and that as she stood there inhaling the clean, woodsy scent of his skin she didn't really want him to move away. "Being poor doesn't mean being dirty. You can still be clean. All it takes is a little soap and water and effort."

Suddenly fidgety and needing something to do, she strode out to the waiting room and began to straighten the magazines. He followed her, lending a hand where he could.

"You surprise me," he said softly, catching her hand when finished. She stood upright again.

"Why?" His touch was warm and all too comforting. Hastily she withdrew her hand and slipped past him to neaten up the toy corner.

"I never pegged you as the maternal type." He shoved his hands in the pockets of his jeans and continued watching her. "I guess I was wrong."

Was that what this was about? Hilary wondered stunned. Was it her biological clock ticking? Heaven knew, back in Boston she'd never had a child's needs weigh on her so heavily as now. "My feelings about motherhood have nothing to do with this," she said stiffly.

"Sure about that?"

She didn't like the way he was challenging her. It made her uncomfortable. "Clementine reminds me of myself at that age, okay?"

"How so?"

"I lost my mother, too, when I was little older than Clem. I remember how much it hurt." She remembered how alone, how bereft she and her sister'd felt. She sensed Clementine felt the same way. It was there in her eyes, the hunger for a woman's touch, for another mother.

Rick was silent. "I'm sorry."

She knew he was, but that didn't change things. She still had to help Clementine. "I'd like to have another talk with the father—"

Rick sighed. He wanted to support her, but he knew she was setting herself up for defeat. Or was she? Thinking long and hard he turned to her. "Wilbur has lived this way all his life. But if this is something you feel you have to do, I'll stand behind you."

TWELVE HOURS LATER she thought she'd found an answer.

"You want to do what?" Rick asked, early the next morning.

Hilary had arranged to drop by to talk to him before work. Since he was going out to the mine that morning and she was manning the clinic, they had elected to talk at his home. Hilary accepted the cup of coffee he offered her and took a seat at his kitchen table. "I want to teach classes in home safety." She winced at the scraping sound Rick's chair made as he dragged it away from the table and slouched down in it. "Why are you looking at me like that?"

He took another long quaff of coffee and shook his head. "Because, Boston, I think you're spinning wheels. First off, who'd come?"

The man was as blunt as she was inventive. "Lots of people would come—if you were teaching it, right alongside me, that is."

Leaning forward, Rick put his elbows on the table and rested his face on his upraised palms. Rubbing at his forehead as if he had a thundering migraine, he asked through a row of perfect white teeth, "Why would I want to do that?"

Hilary sat farther back in her chair and took another sip of his delicious coffee. He wasn't going to discourage her or talk her out of this, no matter how much he tried. "Because you care about the people in this community, and you don't want to see them have senseless accidents.'' She spoke as clearly and carefully as he.

"Senseless accidents," he repeated, shaking his head, as if that would clear it.

She leaned forward and laced her fingers through his, her touch sending a tingle through him. "Rick, my first week here I really wasn't sure if I would be able to do any good, at all. You know the second and third weeks haven't been that much better—in fact, in a lot of ways they've been worse. But my experiences with Mrs. Orlansky and Clementine Morris have changed all that. I know now that there's much for me to do here, especially in terms of the education of the residents. They're not dumb, they just need to be enlightened." She knew it was a tremendous task, but she wanted to try.

Rick withdrew his hand and sat back in the chair. "You're right to think dumping is a problem around here. It is. What you haven't considered is that the people like living exactly the way they do. They don't want to take the broken washers and wrecked cars out of their yards. To them, each car, each washer, has a story or evokes a memory."

She nodded and leaned forward earnestly, "If the people like living that way, it's only because they haven't lived any other way." She could see he was going to argue with her again. She hated the fact he was playing devil's advocate, but she understood.

Instead of arguing he leaned forward and shook his head, a gleam in his eyes. "I must be crazy," he muttered. "Okay. It's worth a try."

Hilary felt exultant. She clacked her cup against his, for a toast. "This is to a worthwhile enterprise . . . partner."

"DECIDING TO OFFER a free dessert smorgasbord after the lecture was a stroke of genius," Becca said to Hilary the following Wednesday evening.

Hilary smiled as yet another citizen added to the tempting array of home-baked confections displayed on the banquet table in the church basement. "A spoonful of sugar always helps the medicine go down."

"I'll second that," Rick Burnett said, coming up to join them. He looked so casual and at ease standing there beside her. It was no wonder she felt comfortable around him, secure. He always made her feel so welcome—even during the rare moments they disagreed.

He continued to regard her with his relaxed, friendly air. "Ready to go?"

Her heartbeat sped up a fraction, but to her credit she kept her voice level, calm as she answered him. "Almost." She bit into her lower lip and turned to him dubiously. "Do you think this is it?"

So far only about fifteen people had shown up. Most were members of the small community church choir, which had been rehearsing earlier that evening, plus Rick's mother, brother and his fiancée, Daisy. Unfortunately people like the Morrises, who needed to be there the most, were nowhere in sight. Hilary tried not to let herself be too discouraged. She had known this would be an uphill battle. She had to start small, if she was going to make a difference.

"Probably," Rick said laconically.

"Uh-oh, here comes trouble," Becca said, as Emma Schwartz sauntered in. Emma glared at Hilary, then took a front-row seat.

Rick looked at Hilary closely to gauge her reaction. She kept her outward cool, though inwardly she still remembered all too well the humiliation she'd felt that day in the clinic, when Emma had called her a quack. Did she plan to do that again tonight? Hilary hoped not. Aware her knees were just a tiny bit shaky, she moved to sit down in one of the folding chairs set up behind the podium.

Rick began with a talk about safety outside the home—in the yard, the garage or workshop. He was very low-key in his approach and had the audience laughing as he recounted stories about his own occasional ineptness. He related injuries other local doctors had seen.

His was a hard act to follow, but Hilary aimed for the same easygoing approach as Rick had used with such success, to demonstrate how to shield yourself from steam when lifting covers from hot pans, and how to turn pot handles away from the stove front so they couldn't be knocked off accidentally.

To her relief, Emma didn't interrupt once during the entire presentation. Everyone was attentive, interested.

Afterward Alva came up to them. "Hilary, wonderful class, wonderful idea. I never knew that about pot handles. I'll have to watch myself."

If one person had learned something that might prevent him from falling victim to a household accident, it was a success. Hilary beamed at Alva's praise. "Just keep yourself safe and healthy."

Rick handed Hilary a slice of coconut cake. Watching the two of them, Alva smiled. Hilary had the unsettling feeling Alva was assuming something that just wasn't true. The assumption made her uncomfortable, and it was all she could do not to squirm under Alva's benevolent gaze. The woman is matchmaking, she thought, just as sure as I'm standing here. And although Rick was a very attractive man, she wasn't looking to complicate her life any more than it already was.

"Kenny's engagement party is the weekend after next," Alva announced pleasantly. "I'd really like you to come."

At the mention of his brother's wedding Rick moved off, ostensibly to talk to someone else. Again Hilary wondered at the tenseness he displayed when-

ever the subject of Kenny's wedding came up. She
would have to ask him when the time was right.

Realizing Alva was still waiting for a response,
Hilary turned back to the friendly older woman. A
party would be a nice diversion. Heaven knew she
needed to spend less time thinking about Rick and
fantasizing about what could never be. Maybe it
would help, too, if she got to know some of the people socially. Maybe then they would trust her more
readily. She smiled at Alva. "I'd like that very much."

"IS IT GOING TO HURT when you take the stitches
out?" Clementine asked Hilary shyly, the following
morning.

Hilary shook her head, glad to have one patient to
treat. "You'll barely feel it." Her manner was as
soothing and reassuring as she could make it, and she
patted the examining table. "Hop up here."

She gave the little girl a hand. As before, Clementine Morris was dressed in grimy clothes. Dirt stained
her hands and face, and even the bandage on her foot
was filthy. An immaculately groomed Daisy stood in
the corner, watching.

Hilary felt a surge of anger, glancing from the me-
ticulously turned-out baby-sitter to the filthy child.
Was this why Rick was opposed to the marriage? Because his brother's fiancée didn't care for little
Clementine as well as one would hope? "So what have
you been doing the past week and a half?" Hilary

asked pleasantly, wanting to take Clementine's mind off the coming procedure.

"Playing, mostly." Clem watched, wide-eyed, as Hilary used surgical scissors to snip off the bandage.

Hilary smiled. "What else?"

"Well . . . Daisy's getting married and she says I get to be her flower girl!" Clementine announced proudly. Unable to sit still, she was so excited, she swung her long dark blond hair around, then twirled a strand between her fingers. It had been so long since her hair had been combed, it looked ratted as if for volume.

Refusing to give in to her own desire to wash the child and find out what she really looked like underneath, Hilary pulled her swivel chair closer to the table. She was a doctor, not a nanny. She had to remember that. If Clementine didn't bathe regularly, it wasn't her concern. Resting Clementine's foot on her thigh, she examined the wound. It had healed nicely, and stayed remarkably clean beneath the plentiful bandage. Carefully Hilary began removing the stitches.

"You're gonna have to get a new dress, though." Daisy glanced at Hilary and explained, "Kenny's mom said she'd make it for her."

"How nice," Hilary said, smiling.

"And you're going to have to get a bath," Daisy continued firmly.

Clem made a face. "I hate baths! Yuck! You know my daddy said I don't have to take one unless I want one. And I don't want one, Daisy, so there!"

"Clementine—" Daisy began tiredly, looking suddenly much older than her eighteen years. Suddenly Hilary knew what the problem really was. Daisy cared about her young charge, she just couldn't make her mind. Hilary had been wrong to blame Daisy for her little cousin's disreputable state. Clearly, Daisy had just been given more responsibility than she could handle.

"Don't be bossy, Daisy," Clementine scolded, then impishly stuck out her tongue at her cousin.

Daisy's pale cheeks turned red. She scowled at Clementine, who was wiggling again and itching at her head, this time with both hands. "Clementine, please, be nice."

Clementine made a comical face, but settled down.

Hilary stood up. "All done." Her glance narrowed to the girl's scalp, as Clementine scratched with even more energy. And suddenly she had an idea what was wrong.

"Let me have a look." Hands on the little girl's shoulders, she moved her around, so her back was to both of them. Looking at her crown, Hilary knew instantly what the problem was. Clementine had lice.

"You mean I got bugs in my hair? Get them out!" Clem cried, as soon as she was told. "Get them out right now!"

Daisy looked like she was ready to faint again. Hilary pushed her into a chair, and then went to the supply room for medication. "You're going to have to sterilize all the bedding and clothes, towels—everything in the trailer she might have rubbed up against," Hilary told Daisy as she donned surgical gloves and then applied a solution to Clementine's scalp and began working it through her hair. "Does Wilbur have a washing machine there?"

Looking relieved to be able to escape the examination room, Daisy nodded. "Yes, I'll get started on it right away."

"There's a box of clothing in the front hall closet. Why don't you go sort through it and see if there's anything Clementine's size. She can borrow something to wear home."

"What's wrong with these clothes?" Clem asked.

"Nothing, except they need to be sterilized, too."

Once the delousing solution had been left on ten minutes, Hilary shampooed Clementine's hair thoroughly with regular shampoo and rinsed it with warm water. Telling herself it was just curiosity—she wanted to see what the little girl looked like clean— Hilary filled the basin with warm water. "Oh, what the heck. As long as we started, we might as well give you the full beauty-shop treatment. Ever played the washing game?"

Clementine looked at her as if she was crazy. And maybe she was, Hilary thought ruefully. She knew she shouldn't be getting this emotionally involved with any patient, never mind a motherless little girl.

"No. What's that?"

Feeling more useful than she had in days, Hilary handed her a washcloth and a bar of soap. "You start with one arm, say from wrist to elbow, and you see just how clean you can make it . . ."

RICK WALKED INTO the clinic, exhausted from an afternoon of making house calls around the county. The waiting room was empty. Not surprising since it was almost six o'clock. What he didn't expect was the sound of soft, feminine laughter coming from Hilary's office, followed by the unmistakable high-pitched laugh of a child.

Curious, he walked in the direction of the sound. The door to her office was open. Hilary was sitting behind her desk, a scrubbed Clementine on the other side. He blinked, amazed at how silky and pale blond the little girl's hair was. He'd always thought it was brown. She was wearing clean clothes, too, and a pair of battered sneakers. Neither her cousin Daisy nor her dad was anywhere in sight.

"What's going on here?" He studied the color in Hilary's face and decided he liked it.

"A red-hot game of Go Fish, that's what." Hilary played a card and glanced up at him. "We're waiting for Daisy to come back and pick up Clementine."

"I had lice!" Clementine announced. "But Dr. Hilary got rid of them, Dr. Rick. And now my head don't itch no more! Isn't that good?"

He couldn't remember ever seeing Clementine so animated. Or happy. He smiled back at her, amazed and grateful. "It sure is."

Hilary frowned with comically exaggerated dismay when Clementine played her next card, then studying the cards in her hand, continued to explain without looking up, "Daisy went back to the trailer to sterilize Clementine's clothing and bed linens. I figured she had her hands full, so I said I'd keep Clementine here with me until she was done."

"I've been a big help, too," Clementine said. "I helped Hilary straighten up her office and mop the floor—" Clementine giggled again. "I made a big mess with the soap while's I was getting my bath."

It was worth it. Rick glanced at Hilary, surprised she had done the delousing herself. She could've just sent Daisy home with instructions. She probably would have, had she been back in Boston. But she had changed since coming to Kentucky, become warmer, more open, more trusting of those around her. If only she could stay, he thought wistfully, become a permanent part of his life. But he knew, even as he thought it, it was too much to ask.

Just then the front door opened and Daisy walked in, keys in hand. She did a double take when she got a look at Clem. "My gosh, honey, you're beautiful!"

"I am, ain't I?" Giggling and preening, Clem struck a movie-star pose.

Hilary got up to give Daisy another bottle of liquid, along with a fine-toothed comb. She explained directions, then bent to Clementine's level. "I want you to promise me you'll be good when Daisy washes your head with this solution again tomorrow, okay? It's important you not get any in your eyes."

"Okay." Clementine's lower lip stuck out petulantly.

Rick had to work to suppress a smile.

"Will you come back and see me?" Hilary asked, tenderly smoothing Clementine's silky hair from her face.

Clementine nodded enthusiastically. "Maybe we can play cards some time!"

Hilary bent and impulsively kissed her goodbye. "Maybe."

As the two girls left, Rick lapsed into bemused silence. It was silly, but he couldn't help but wonder how it would feel to be on the receiving end of Hilary's affection. She had so much to give...

Once the girls were gone, Hilary's bright facade faded with remarkable speed.

Rick wondered what was on her mind. Relishing the quiet of the clinic, he sat down opposite her and propped his feet on the corner of her desk. "Something bothering you?"

She gave him an even look that had nothing to do with where he'd put his feet. "That little girl never should have had lice."

Rick returned his feet to the floor and sat forward. "I agree, Hilary. But remember, around here many houses still don't have indoor plumbing."

"But Clementine's does," she said, rising to her feet. "I've got half a mind to call Wilbur Morris and tell him what I think!"

Rick was alarmed. He knew she was suffering from feeling that she had been too removed in the Jones case. But that invisible line that separated every patient and physician was there for a reason. It protected them both. Failures were inevitable and keeping to the line was the smartest move.

"Hilary, think," he soothed. "If you do, you'll never see Clementine again."

Hilary fell silent, her anguish rising. "Rick—" She paced the office restlessly, reminding him of a storm cloud about to burst.

Giving in to impulse, he touched her shoulder lightly as she passed. She turned to face him. Her face was tilted up to his. "Clementine is going to be fine," he said. "I think half of what's going on with her now reflects a tomboy stage. She'll get over it. With your help, even sooner."

Hilary sighed, her eyes still holding his.

Realizing Hilary wasn't the only one getting too involved here, Rick dropped his hold on her. "You okay?"

Hilary nodded slowly. "I haven't changed my mind, though. I still think something should be done."

Rick leaned against the wall, admiring her purity of spirit. He had lost his a lifetime ago. "You think life could and should be perfect and good for everyone, don't you?" On one hand, her attitude seemed admirable. On another, almost childlike in her naïveté.

She whirled to face him, her expression fierce, determined. "Yes, I do." She faced him in silence. Slowly, recognition dawned on her face. "You're telling me you don't?"

Wishing there was a less blunt way to say this and still get his message across, he thrust his hands into his pockets. "I've known poverty all my life, Hil. It doesn't shock me. Or even repel me. It just . . . is."

"I've seen poverty, too, and I think dignity's important."

He fell silent. For the first time he understood what a deeply compassionate person she was, at heart.

He let out a long breath and moved away from the wall. As he neared her, he saw her lower lip tremble and for the barest fraction of a second, he thought how soft, kissable her mouth looked. "Look, Hilary, I share your frustration in this area, but we have to be realistic here. This region needs doctors who'll be there for them, good or bad.''

She moved away from him. "I'm tired," she said abruptly. "I'm going home."

"Hil—" He didn't want them to part this way, no closer than before. But she was giving them no choice.

"Good night, Rick." She moved past him and headed for the door. Her footsteps faded as she walked down the hall toward the exit.

For a second he was tempted to go after her, but in the end he decided to hold his ground. He felt she would think about things, let them sink in and maybe come up with some fresh ideas. If anything, she had started him thinking.

Chapter Six

"Talk about a backwoods aura. You really are out in the boonies, aren't you?"

Hilary looked up from the medical journal she had been reading, to see her lifelong friend and attorney standing in the doorway. Dash Barrington. As she took in his handsome visage, surprise mingled with delight. Warning or no, she was very glad to see him; her friendship with Dash and his wife, Cara, dated back to her elementary-school days. She rose excitedly, circling around the front of her desk. "Dash, hi—"

Setting his briefcase on the floor, he crossed the room to give her a warm hug. For a moment, they embraced wordlessly. She was flooded with familial warmth. Her father had died two years ago, and Dash and Cara were now the closest thing to family that she had. She needed them both more than ever.

Releasing her, he let his eyes skim over her, then murmured satisfaction. "Well, you seem to be all in one piece."

He was dressed in his usual attire: a classic navy blazer, white slacks, white shirt and striped navy tie. He looked very urbane, sophisticated—in direct contrast to her casual state.

"Jeans to work?" He raised a skeptical brow.

A few months ago she would have been shocked, too. "Everyone here wears them." Although hers alone carried a Guess label. She smiled at her old friend, admitting unabashedly, "I've been trying to fit in." Her brow furrowed as the miracle of his presence, and the sheer surprise of it, sank in. "What are you doing here, anyway?"

He shrugged, as if flying a thousand miles to see her was of no consequence at all. "First and foremost, checking up on you. Cara and I've been worried. You sounded a little down the last couple of times we spoke, even though you wouldn't own up to it."

"I know. I'm sorry." She hadn't wanted to indulge herself in self-pity. Although she had tried to hide her unhappiness, she should have guessed, as close as they were, that Dash and Cara would pick up on it.

"Don't apologize. You have every right to feel discouraged and depressed, right now. Anyone in your place would."

It helped, hearing him say it. Still, she knew there had to be more than he'd revealed thus far. Dash never did anything without a solid reason. "Is that the only reason you're here?"

He shook his head, "No, actually, it's not. I wanted to have a look around for myself, see what kind of environment you're operating in. We might be able to use it to our advantage in the trial."

A chill went through her at the calculated nature of his words. She knew it was his business to protect her, in any and every way that he could, but it was disconcerting to realize how very far Dash had come to do so. "I don't get it," she said slowly. "How would my being here work to our advantage?"

Feeling the heat in the tiny office, Dash loosened his tie and began to pace. "Mrs. Jones's attorneys will be trying to portray you as incompetent, uncaring. It's our job to show the jury otherwise. We've already got character witnesses and other physicians such as Dr. Whitfield from Boston General to testify on your behalf. But I was thinking if we could count on some people here, our case would be strengthened." He stopped and smiled. "Have you done anything even remotely heroic since you've been here?"

Hilary saw where this was going, and she didn't like it. She didn't want to be turned into some kind of saint or martyr. "You're kidding, aren't you?"

His eyes met hers. Dash shook his head, his regret showing. "I only wish I were, kiddo. The way things look now, you'll need every bit of help you can get."

A chill of foreboding went down her spine. "It's that bad?" she asked hoarsely.

Dash sidestepped her question adroitly. "Let's just say we could use the boost. Have you done anything that would look good in court?"

Hilary felt her jaw set. "No."

"And—?" he prompted, seeing there was more to come than she was saying.

As much as she hated to argue—with anyone— Hilary knew she had to speak her mind. "I don't like it, Dash. This self-aggrandizing promotion you're describing seems dishonest . . . I don't know."

He didn't think so. "We'd only be telling the truth."

"A truth that uses others' goodwill."

He lifted his hands helplessly, his attitude nonchalant. "Think of it as a way to balance the scales. The plaintiff's attorneys will be trying to discredit you."

Hilary swallowed uneasily. "I think my reputation at Boston General is above reproach. Colleagues and patients will be supportive."

"True. But it doesn't hurt to get support from patients you've treated since the suit."

She sighed. "Maybe you're right. I'll think about it."

Dash looked around. "This is a big step down from your office at Boston General." He turned back to her, his gaze narrowing shrewdly. "You must miss it."

She shrugged, not so sure anymore. "I'm adjusting," she said lightly.

He shook his head in mute remonstration. "I couldn't. Not if my life depended on it, I don't think."

Dash frowned contemplatively. After a moment, he brightened. "We could use the philanthropic nature of this job as support. The fact you were willing to take it at all is to your advantage."

She shrugged. "If the plaintiff's attorneys don't point out it was the only job I could get under such short notice."

His eyes darkened. "'Under short notice' is the key phrase here," he countered sternly. "Let's try and take a positive attitude in this thing, okay?"

At his pleading tone, Hilary looked up and smiled. "Okay. You're right. I do appreciate your ideas on my behalf, Dash. I'll try to cooperate. But I'll have to think about names. Give me time."

He took the chair in front of her desk and sat down lazily. "That's the spirit. Okay. For now I'll resort to your Boston associates. If I see a need for others— here—I'll give you a call."

She nodded.

"So...on a more personal note...how are you faring?"

"Fine, Dash," she said. She was slowly gaining new patients. A few came now just to see her at the clinic. That morning she'd made six house calls on elderly shut-ins, including Mrs. Orlansky. All had been grateful for the company and seemed to set store by her medical expertise. She was happy to keep busy while being useful to others.

"Just fine?"

Hilary shrugged, trying hard to contain the hurt she felt at having to win over "doubting Thomas" patients. If it weren't for the Jones case... "There's a lot to get used to."

He nodded in affirmation, still studying her with a lawyer's eagle eye. "I guess. You're not doing any obstetrical work, are you—not even on the QT? Because that could really jeopardize your case, you know."

"I'm being prudent, Dash. I swear." More than anything, she wanted to get back to delivering babies full time. Her fear of doing so hadn't entirely disappeared; but her confidence in her general medical skills was fast coming back.

"It must be hard for you, not to be delivering babies now."

He knew firsthand how much she loved it—she had delivered Dash and Cara's first child. Hilary refused to think about it and changed the subject smoothly. "Why didn't you let me know you were coming? I would've picked you up at the airport."

Dash shrugged, as if it were of no consequence. "That's okay. I didn't want you to go to any trouble. I'm on my way to visit a client in West Virginia and a stop here was easy enough."

"That's a relief, you doubling up business."

"Hey, what are old friends for?"

She smiled. She had missed Dash and Cara and her other Boston cronies. She sobered, though, as she thought about the other probable reasons behind his visit. "So how's my defense going?" she prompted.

"I was getting to that," Dash said, opening his briefcase. "I hit on something, and I need to know if it means anything. I found out Mrs. Jones missed several days of work in the first four months of pregnancy, due to illness. A couple were in the first month, one halfway through the second month, and the last one in the week before she miscarried, coincidentally a day or so before she came in to see you." Dash withdrew several papers and handed them to her. "I didn't see any notes about it in your records on the case. I wondered if you remembered what was going on."

Hilary glanced at the data he had gathered. Slowly her frown deepened. "No, I don't know anything about this." She looked at him, bewildered. "Have you talked to Mrs. Jones?"

"No. I wanted to talk to you first. Is it possible she could have called and you just forgot?"

Hilary shook her head. "No. Every time a patient calls in and talks to me her file is pulled and the call logged. Had she called in at all, there would have been a note on her chart." Hilary paused, her mind racing. Was it possible Mrs. Jones had suffered some symptoms, some cramping or bleeding, and simply not told

Hilary about them—or ignored the symptoms in the hope they would go away? If that was the case, it would mean she wasn't guilty of malpractice. She glanced up, feeling mildly encouraged for the first time in months. "Are you going to talk to Mrs. Jones about this?"

Dash shook his head and glanced at his watch. "Why don't we break? I'll drive us into Lexington for a quick bite to eat. We can discuss strategy there."

Hilary felt energetic. "It'll be on me."

THE NEXT MORNING she met Rick at the mine. The company was ready to hire twenty-five more workers and physicals had to be done on the applicants.

Hilary had slept well after the conversation with her lawyer. She had also spent time trying to figure out how to get along with Emma Schwartz, who operated an office at the mine for the EPA.

So once at the mine the next morning, Hilary wasted no time in going to see her adversary. "Emma, can I talk to you a moment?"

Emma looked up, frankly shocked. Hilary was relieved to see the woman was in fairly good health, with slightly less edema than she had evidenced the last time she had seen her.

Emma inclined her head, indicating Hilary could come in if she liked. She had heard some of the recent praise of Hilary's ability, and she had dismissed the stories as "hogwash." "If you're here to plead your case with me—" Emma began warily.

"It has nothing to do with our previous discussion," Hilary said quietly. "I know you work for the Environmental Protection Agency. And I want to tell you I've heard the reforesting of strip-mined areas is just wonderful."

"I think so, too."

"But there's a lot more that needs to be done around here to preserve the environment."

Emma sat up straighter and put down her pen. "What do you mean?"

"You've probably noticed the trash that accumulates in people's yards out here. Glass bottles, tin cans, old newspapers, cars that don't run—"

"Even old kitchen sinks," Emma said, cracking a smile. She shook her head in exasperation and rolled her eyes.

"I'd like to see something done about that."

Emma shrugged and pushed back her chair. "So would I, but short of changing the culture here, I don't see how we can succeed."

Hilary was aware she was still being scrutinized from head to toe. She also felt she'd chinked Emma's armor. "Have any efforts been made to start recycling centers in this area?"

Emma relaxed cautiously. "I don't know. There are centers in all the major cities in the state, but there hasn't been enough money to start any centers here. Nor any interest expressed, I might add.''

"Well, what if we were to try to do it on a volunteer basis?"

Emma made a humorless sound. "It'd probably be about as successful as your home-safety classes."

Ouch, Hilary thought. Emma had heard scuttlebutt. Some residents had been amused by her efforts, but many others had found the courses useful. "Those are going to be continued once a month, and by request. We have enough attendance."

Emma frowned. "Five people?"

"I have to try," Hilary explained. "I want to do my part. I would think you would, too."

Silence fell between them, less combative this time. "In reference to the recycling..." Emma said brusquely at last. She sighed, admitting, "I'm all for preserving the beauty of the environment and so are my friends, so...I'm willing to listen." She pushed her chair closer to her desk again. "What are you proposing?"

"I was hoping that maybe if we worked together we could get local businesses to act as collection sites." Emma's interest perked up and Hilary continued enthusiastically, "Maybe if people could get back some money for their trash, they'd be less likely to dump it in their front yards. You know how poor the area is. A dollar here or there may not seem like much to someone with a steady paycheck coming in, but to some little kid with no other means of support, it might mean a whole month's supply of bubble gum.''

Emma pursed her lips together thoughtfully. ''Actually we could go one better. Offer one-hundred-dollar prizes for anyone who participates in our recycling efforts on a monthly basis. They've done that in other cities. It works.''

''Sounds good to me, but where would we get the money?''

''Leave that to me. I know some private donors who might be enticed to act as sponsors.''

Satisfied she'd accomplished what she'd set out to do, Hilary got up to go.

Emma's voice stopped her at the door. ''You going to see patients today?''

Hilary nodded. She had three on her roster, and knew that Emma felt as protective of her people as she did of the environment. She hoped the other woman would see that medicine was not as black-and-white as other issues.

For a long moment, Emma didn't say anything. Hilary held her breath, hoping Emma would let it go. Finally, reluctantly, she did.

''I'll talk to the agency about how to organize and then get back to you.''

Hilary nodded, immensely relieved, anxious to get out of there. ''You can reach me at the clinic days, at home most evenings.'' Deciding she'd risked trouble long enough, she left Emma's office as quickly and quietly as she'd come.

Hilary found Rick in the infirmary.

"Go okay?" She nodded. He didn't want to press, so they turned their attention to the physicals. Rick worked in one examining room of the infirmary. Hilary another. She was almost finished when Rick's younger brother, Kenny, came in. He looked very nervous. She, too, was taken aback. "Kenny, I didn't expect to see you here today. Are you going to work here?"

"If I pass my physical." Reading her confusion, Kenny said, "Rick doesn't know."

Hilary's heart skipped a beat. She didn't want to be in the midst of a quarrel between the two brothers. "Don't you think you should tell him?"

"He wouldn't approve, Hilary."

Hilary thought of the physical toll taken on the mine workers. They aged prematurely and risked developing life-shortening diseases such as black lung. "I'm not sure I do, either," she said quietly.

"Promise me you won't—"

Without warning, Rick stuck his head in the door. "Hil, I need a second...Kenny." He did a double take, his face turning very white. "What are you doing here?"

Kenny took a deep breath, his spine stiffening. "Same as everyone else. Getting a physical. I plan to start work next week."

Rick stared at him incredulously. "You can't work here."

"The pay is good, Rick. Three to four times what I'd get anywhere else. If I worked here I'd be able to put Daisy through school."

His expression grim Rick shut the door behind him, enclosing them all inside the tiny room. "Kenny, I know the money sounds good, but stop a minute. Really think about what you're doing."

Kenny's jaw tightened. "I have."

Rick shook his head in mute disapproval. "Mom will be torn up when she finds out."

"She already knows."

Silence. Rick's teeth clenched. "I can't believe she wants this for you," he said hoarsely, the hurt he felt at having been excluded from all discussions showing on his face.

"At least she understands I have a right to make my own decisions," Kenny shot back angrily.

"I don't want you to do this," Rick enunciated plainly.

"Like I said before, you don't have any say in it," Kenny shot back, just as determinedly.

Rick glanced at Hilary, then turned and walked out of the room. Hilary's heart was pounding. She knew Rick wanted her to find some reason Kenny would be unable to work in the mine. Unfortunately as it turned out he was in perfect health. Nevertheless, knowing how his brother felt about Kenny working there, it wasn't easy for her to sign the papers stating his eligibility health-wise.

She didn't see Rick again until they got ready to leave the mine. He opened the door for her and followed her out, then fell into step beside her. "Sorry about that scene with my brother," he said gruffly, looking even more upset than he had before.

"I know how you feel," she said softly, stopping next to his truck, touching his arm. "If I were in your place, I'd feel the same way."

Rick released a long breath. She was backed up against the passenger door of his truck and he rested an arm on the frame next to her shoulder. "He won't listen to anything I say."

"Then I guess you're going to have to let him make his own mistakes."

"Dammit, though, it's so self-destructive."

"Right now, Rick, it's the healthiest thing he can do for himself and Daisy."

Hilary fell silent. She felt cossetted between the warmth of his body and the sun-warmed metal behind her. Knowing how upset he was, it was all she could do not to take him into her arms and just hold him, offer him what little comfort she could. Knowing, however, how that was likely to be misconstrued, if not by Rick then by the mine workers milling about on the grounds, she remained stiffly in place.

Rick passed a hand over his eyes. After a moment, he composed himself and moved slightly back, away from her. When he looked at her, it was with a mixture of friendship and gratitude. And something else...she couldn't quite identify.

"You're right, of course," he murmured gently. "Thanks for the advice."

"Any time," Hilary said softly. She just wished she could have done more.

"YOU DIDN'T HAVE TO pick me up for the party, you know," Hilary said as she greeted Rick at the door the following Saturday evening. She opened the screen door and turned sideways, so he could pass. Although she knew he was still upset about his brother taking the job in the coal mine, he had not talked about it since, and didn't appear to want to take up the conversation. She was content, therefore, to concentrate on acting as if everything was normal. If she had a task, it was to try and keep his spirits up. Besides, Kenny seemed like such an outdoorsy person. She couldn't believe he would be content to work in the mine for very long. No, probably within a month or two, he would go back to doing farm work or hiring out for odd jobs, and this brouhaha with his brother would all be a thing of the past. In the meantime, she would help Rick get through it, the same way he had helped her through her first rough weeks there in southeastern Kentucky.

She smiled at him drily, relating in a voice that was almost but not quite flirtatious, "I'm perfectly capable of driving myself to your mother's house."

"Yeah? Well, I know that, but Mom doesn't." Rick grinned as he stepped past the small stack of newspapers awaiting recycling on her front porch. The door shut. His glance came back to her. His eyes skimmed the length of her, taking in every powdered, perfumed inch. "She, uh, felt you should have a proper male escort."

From the way he looked at her, she felt like she needed a bodyguard—to keep her safe from Rick. "So you were drafted." It was warm inside the house, despite the window fan she'd turned on full blast.

Rick didn't seem to notice the closeness of the air. He looked cool and comfortable in the tailored khaki shirt and pleated black trousers. He wore no tie, in honor of the occasion. He had shaved, and the familiar deep pine scent of his after-shave clung to his jaw. His hair was as tousled and soft looking as always.

"Hil, let's get this straight. If I'd minded, I wouldn't have come."

His announcement was soft and casual; yet it hit her like an arrow to the heart. She didn't want him to want to be with her. Okay, maybe she did. For ego's sake. But not for reality. The reality was she was leaving ASAP, the moment her lawsuit was settled and her malpractice insurance reinstated. She couldn't forget that, couldn't get sidetracked.

She turned away from him, figuring if he didn't look so damned handsome she wouldn't be acting like such a loon. Her back to him, she said airily, "Make yourself at home. I'm almost ready. Today's been a little crazy." That was the understatement of the year.

He looked pointedly at the moving cartons in her living room, then said drily, "I guess so."

She had worked like crazy since her stuff had arrived to set up her television, VCR and stereo in the living room. Her microwave had been added to the kitchen. Additionally, there were throw pillows and a matching rose-and-white afghan and several framed prints to spruce up the place.

Rick looked around approvingly, his gaze lingering on the fresh-cut wildflowers in the vase on the kitchen table, the new coat of ecru paint on the ceiling and walls. "It's beginning to look like a home—"

"And not just a temporary residence? I know." Hilary sighed her satisfaction as she fastened on an earring. "Even though I'll only be here a short while, I wanted a sense of permanency here. I wanted to belong. Does that make any sense?"

He nodded, looking not as happy as he had just moments earlier. His glance scanned her navy calico halter-style sundress with the white lace collar. The summery dress left her shoulders and upper back bare, the full skirt falling in soft folds to mid-calf. "New dress?"

Hilary nodded, aware her heart was beating a tad faster. Following the fashion of other women in the area, she had decided not to wear panty hose with the white sandals she had purchased to go with the dress. Growing up, she'd been taught a lady never went bare-legged in a dress. But it was so hot and humid the past few days, she had opted for comfort instead.

Rick's glance lingered momentarily where her dress nipped in at the waist before he glanced at his watch and said, a tad impatiently, "We better get going if we don't want to be late."

Once en route Hilary felt the need to fill up the silence with idle chatter. "Is your mom excited about Kenny's wedding?" she asked.

"That, and a little sad. He's her baby. I think it will be odd for her not having anyone to fuss over."

Again Hilary detected the reservation, the hint of worry in Rick's voice, and wondered about it. "She probably didn't expect him to get married this soon, did she?" Kenny was only eighteen, and although he seemed mature for his age, Hilary couldn't help but think how young that was to be making a commitment that would last a lifetime.

"No, none of us did," Rick said tersely. "In fact, I tried to talk him out of it, but he's of legal age here in Kentucky, so there's not much I can do to stop him."

"Except talk to him."

"I have. So has Mom. It didn't work."

"I'm sorry. What are their plans after the wedding?"

Rick sighed. "That's another bone of contention. Daisy has a partial scholarship to Pikeville College. She wants to be a teacher. Kenny's decided to help put her through school, rather than go to college himself."

Now Hilary saw why Rick was so worried. She swiveled to face him, as much as her seat belt would allow. "You're afraid he'll never go, aren't you?"

Rick nodded, his expression grim. "I know it's his life. I know he has the right to make his own decisions, but I can't help thinking he's making a mistake."

"Does Kenny know that?"

"Yep. Not that he cares." Rick guided his truck into the driveway leading to his mother's house. Cars were parked on either side of the large spacious yard. People spilled out on the porch and into the yard.

Rick cut the motor. He turned to her, resting his arm along the seat behind her. "Do you think I'm being overprotective?"

Hilary glanced at the happy couple. Daisy and Kenny were up on the front porch, holding court. Daisy looked ravishingly beautiful in a sky-blue cotton dress. Kenny was also in his Sunday best, his hair neatly parted on the side. They were holding hands. Watching them, she knew a moment's envy. She wanted that for herself, too.

Aware Rick was waiting for an answer from her, she said, softly, "I don't know if you're being overprotective or not, but if it's any comfort, in your place I know I'd feel the same. I'd want them to be older before they took such a big step. On the other hand, they look happy. I want to believe everything will work out for them."

"So do I," Rick said quietly.

Hilary looked up at him. He was such a kind, loving man. Devoted to family, friends. She was glad she'd gotten the chance to know him better.

"Well, I'd better circulate," he said, moving away reluctantly.

"Hi, Dr. Hilary." Clementine Morris interrupted cheerfully, appearing at her side. She too had recently had a bath. Her pale blond hair was clean and silky-looking. "Do you like my dress?" Clementine twirled around on tiptoe. "Alva made my dress and she made Daisy's, too! Out of the same material."

"I can see that, and you both look very pretty."

"Daisy took me to get my hair cut, too. She says she'll take me again, if I remember to keep it clean."

Hilary smiled approvingly. It seemed Daisy was finally learning how to manage her young charge. She wondered who would care for the rambunctious little girl when Daisy went away to school.

Across the yard, Rick was talking to a pretty young woman. Coming up beside her Alva noticed the direction of Hilary's gaze and said, "That's one of

Rick's patients. He helped her through a bad time last year when her husband died.''

A surge of emotion went through Hilary. Telling herself it was ridiculous, she pushed the unfamiliar feeling aside. ''Rick's a very kind man,'' she said to Alva, irritated at herself for feeling such a powerful emotion. *I have no claim on him.*

His mother nodded. ''That's probably what makes him such a good doctor. He has such empathy for people, especially those in trouble.''

Me included, Hilary thought, disturbed. Was that what she was to Rick, another charity case, someone he had to be kind to? It hurt her to think that might be true.

Well, in any case, there was only one thing for her to do now, and that was enjoy herself. With a determined smile, Hilary set out to circulate.

It surprised her, how many people she knew there. Perhaps it was the party, the festive mood, but it seemed everyone went out of their way to make her feel welcome, and the rest of the party was a jovial affair. Clementine ran in and out of the house with other cousins. Daisy had eyes for no one but Kenny, and vice versa.

The highlight of the evening was when they opened gifts. Daisy's parents had given them a handmade quilt in a wedding-ring design, sewn by every member of her family. Alva gave them a crocheted afghan. But it was Rick's gift to the happy couple Hilary found most interesting. It was a handcrafted wooden decoupage plaque, made in the design of a family tree. At the top was a wedding photo from their parents' wedding, and another of Daisy's parents' wedding. There was a place for Kenny and Daisy's wedding photo, and other spaces for the children they would someday have. It was beautiful and sentimental. She could tell he'd spent a long time working on it.

"That was a lovely gift you gave your brother and his fiancée," she said, the first chance she got. Rick was sitting at a picnic table out in the backyard, away from the crowd inside.

"Thanks." Taking her hand in his, he pulled her down to sit beside her.

His brows knitting together worriedly, he looked at her for confirmation. "They liked it, didn't they?"

So absorbed at looking at him was she, she completely lost the thread of the conversation. "Liked what?"

His mouth lifted in a wry grin. "The gift."

"Oh. Yes." She smiled and tugged her skirt even farther down over her knees. "Everyone did."

He studied her a moment longer, then went back to stargazing. He raised a hand to rub at the back of his neck, then dropped it abruptly when he found her staring again. "I wasn't sure about using the photos of our parents," he continued easily, still watching her in the same, almost too casual manner, "but then I thought it would probably mean more if I did. Not that Kenny remembers Dad very well, anyway." Rick shrugged. "He died when Kenny was just four."

Hilary knew how it felt to lose a parent, and her heart went out to them. It occurred to her then, as his vulnerability settled like an ache in her chest, how close she was beginning to feel to him and how little she still knew about what he was thinking and feeling. "How old were you when your dad died?" she asked quietly.

Rick turned to face her, the memory of his grief stamped in the lines of his face. "Twenty-one. I had just finished final exams when I got word that he had collapsed in the mine. I got home right away, but his stroke was too severe to hope for a recovery. He died a couple of weeks later, without ever coming out of it."

He paused as if struggling for breath. It was a few moments before he went on in a raspy voice, "You know it's funny. I never knew how much I counted on my dad being around until he was gone. It was hardest on my mom, of course. In a lot of ways, he was her life."

"Do you think your dad would be happy if he were here today?" Hilary ventured after a moment, unsure how he would take such a personal question.

Rick shrugged, the troubled light coming back into his light gray eyes. "I don't know," he said softly, pushing away from the picnic bench. He walked out into the yard, and motioned for her to follow. "I know he wanted both of us to go to college, but he also felt everyone should be able to follow his own dream." He turned to face her, his nearness sending her senses reeling.

He touched a hand to the side of her face.

Her heart began to beat a little faster. Unsure where this was going, what he wanted from her, she struggled to keep the conversation going. "I admire them for having the guts to make the commitment. It's a big step."

"Yes, it is," he said softly, linking his hand with hers.

His touch was warm, magnetic. She longed to lean into him, to give in to the kiss she felt was coming, but she also worried about the future.

She stepped back slightly, withdrawing her hands from his light, easy grip. He looked at her, questioning and waiting. Wanting.

Her throat was so dry she could barely speak. "What about you?" she said lightly, remembering that when he had been in Boston he had been romantically involved with someone back home. "Have you ever been married?"

His eyes gently searched hers, but he stayed his ground. "No. I was engaged once, but that's it."

Hilary's chest felt even tighter. "What happened?" Her voice sounded tense, husky, even to her own ears. She couldn't imagine anyone not wanting to marry Rick.

A shadow crossed his face. "She didn't want to live in Appalachia." He said it so simply, yet his words barely concealed a mountain of hurt. "She thought after living in Boston for three years I'd change my mind and want to stay on there—or at least move to a city where I could start my own practice. I didn't, and she couldn't accept that."

Hilary felt for him. If anyone deserved rejection less, it was Rick. "I'm sorry."

He shrugged as if the matter was of no consequence, and walked a little further out into the yard, a little further from the lights and the gaiety still emanating from the house. "Don't be. It worked out for the best, I'm sure. Had she stayed here out of a sense of duty when she was so anxious to get out of Appalachia, I'm sure we both would have been miserable." He slanted her a curious look. "What about you? Have you ever been married or anything?"

Hilary shook her head. "I came close a couple of times but...no. I was never engaged, never married."

"Never in love?"

"No." She had hoped for it, though. One of these days she wanted to get married, settle down.

Without warning in the distance there was a sharp childlike scream. Rick released her. In tandem, they moved toward the sound.

Doors slammed. A child was crying. Guests came spilling out of the house, but Rick and Hilary sprinted round the front and got there first.

Clementine was lying on the ground, her right leg twisted at a funny angle beneath her. "Ouch," she said, crying so hard she could barely catch her breath. "Ouch, I hurt...."

"FORTUNATELY, it's just a sprain," Rick told Wilbur Morris an hour later. Beckoning him to the lighted screen next to the clinic's X-ray machine, he showed Wilbur the pictures of Clementine's ankle. "You see, there's no break in the bone, not even a hairline crack."

Clementine lay on the examining table, her injured left foot wrapped in an Ace bandage, propped up on a pillow and cushioned by ice. It was already swelling. "I want Daisy," Clementine said.

Wilbur turned to his daughter. He crossed to her and took her hand in his, clasping it gently. "Honey, you can see Daisy tomorrow. Thank God for her, though. I don't know what I'd do without her this summer. She's been one big help to me."

And to Clementine, Hilary thought.

"Let me help you get her out to your truck," Rick said.

When he came back in seconds later, Hilary had tidied up. Rick glanced at his watch. "Party's probably over by now. Guess I better drive you home."

Hilary nodded, trying not to feel too disappointed that the evening had come to an end.

"You had a good time tonight, didn't you?" Rick said as he pulled the truck into her drive and cut the motor.

"Yes, I did."

"But it surprises you," he said softly, curiously. "Why?"

"I don't know," Hilary said, pushing from the truck and watching as he circled around to join her. They fell into step together. "I guess because I've never been to anything like that before. I mean, half the local populace was at that party tonight." Trying not to be so aware of his closeness or the tantalizing fragrance of his after-shave, she dug through her purse for her house key.

"We're a close-knit group."

"Yes, you are." She paused to look up. "And like it or not, it takes time to get accepted." She didn't know where that thought had come from. She was appalled she'd spoken it out loud.

"That's true, but you're also a very likable person, with a growing number of friends. Word is spreading, and many came up to speak to you." He slanted her a curious glance and leaned one shoulder against the door frame. "Does that bother you—that we are such a tight group?"

As he waited for her answer, Hilary found it hard to look away. He was so handsome standing there in the soft glow of the porch light, so masculine and warm and giving. Everything she'd ever thought she wanted in a man. And yet by virtue of the circumstances, he was off-limits to her.

Aware he was still waiting for an answer to his question, she shrugged, "It's just not what I'm used to." Not wanting to get any closer to him—or become another of his "charity cases," such as that young woman she'd seen him talking to earlier in the evening—she opened the door and stepped inside.

"What are you used to, then?" he asked, following her inside. "What was your childhood like?"

Taken aback, Hilary put her key back in her purse and put both on the table next to the door. "I grew up in a quiet suburban neighborhood of Boston." He seemed to want more from her, so she elaborated, "We had nice neighbors, but everyone kept pretty much to themselves. There wasn't a lot of interaction. No block parties or anything." Nervous now that he was inside with her, she began picking up a little, putting smaller-sized moving boxes into large ones.

He followed her around, helping her restore order without being asked. "Did your parents entertain a lot?"

She bumped into him as they both reached for the same box. He let her have it. "No, not that I remember," she answered him frankly. "Of course, my mother died when I was six. Heart disease. I remember missing her a lot. My sister and I both did."

Rick's gaze softened. "What about your dad?"

Hilary wished her relationship with him had been better. She struggled to control the regret in her voice. "He was a very proper man. I didn't see a lot of him." She picked up the last stray box, and because it wouldn't fold into any of the others, busied herself dismantling and folding it back up. "His work as a salesman required that he travel a lot." It was a pat answer, but the only one she was truly comfortable with.

"What about when he was home?"

Hilary was silent, trying to remember the few stilted memories she'd had of her dad. "He loved me, I know that, but he had a hard time expressing it. He—we talked mostly about my achievements—good grades, academic awards, stuff like that."

"It sounds lonely."

It had been. And it had gone even farther downhill after her sister's death.

Refusing to feel sorry for herself, she moved away from his sympathetic gaze, and soft, understanding eyes. She didn't want to talk about this any more. Knowing she didn't want the evening to end on this note, she said, "Would you like a cup of coffee? If you want, we could watch a movie on the VCR—or part of one?" A glance at her watch told her it was getting kind of late.

He grinned knowingly. "You miss your HBO, don't you?"

PEEK-A-BOO!

Free Gifts For You!

Look inside—Right Now!
We've got something
special just for you!

U-H-AR-11/90

GIFTS

There's no cost—and no obligation to buy anything!

We'd like to send you free gifts to thank you for being a romance reader, and to introduce you to the benefits of the Harlequin Reader Service®: free home delivery of brand-new Harlequin American Romance® novels months before they're available in stores, and at a savings from the cover price!

Accepting our free gifts places you under no obligation to buy anything ever. You may cancel the Reader Service at any time, even just after receiving your free gifts, simply by writing "cancel" on your statement or returning a shipment of books to us at our cost. But if you choose not to cancel, every month we'll send you four more Harlequin American Romance® novels, and bill you just $2.74* apiece—and there's **no** extra charge for shipping and handling. There are **no** hidden extras!

*Terms and prices subject to change without notice. Sales tax applicable in N.Y. Offer limited to one per household and not valid to current Harlequin American Romance® subscribers.

GALORE

Behind These Doors!

WE EVEN PAY THE POSTAGE!

It costs you nothing to send for your free gifts—we've paid the postage on the attached reply card. And we'll pay the postage on your free gift shipment. We charge nothing for delivery!

BUSINESS REPLY MAIL
FIRST CLASS MAIL   PERMIT NO. 717   BUFFALO, NY

POSTAGE WILL BE PAID BY ADDRESSEE

HARLEQUIN READER SERVICE
3010 WALDEN AVE
PO BOX 1867
BUFFALO NY 14240-9952

NO POSTAGE
NECESSARY
IF MAILED
IN THE
UNITED STATES

She groaned. "I only wish I had the money for a satellite dish." Needing to rid them of the intimacy that had opened between them, she flipped on yet another light and headed for the kitchen. "I'll put the coffee on. The tapes are in the box on top of my desk. Go ahead and look through them."

Realizing as an afterthought that he would need scissors to open the box, she grabbed a pair and returned to the living room seconds later. Rick was standing beside the desk. He hadn't touched the box of tapes. He was looking down at a stack of papers on her desk. For a moment, she couldn't think what could have upset him so—and he was upset, she could tell from the look on his face. And then she remembered.

He held up the half-finished resignation letter she had written days before. Written and never thrown away. "You were really going to leave?" he asked hoarsely, the disbelief he felt showing on his face.

Hilary felt warmth flood her cheeks and then leave just as swiftly. Lord, she was so embarrassed. "I thought about it," she mumbled defensively.

"Why?" Putting the paper down, he came toward her. Half angry, half wanting to understand.

"Because I'm really not wanted here," Hilary said stiffly. A shiver coursed down her spine and she hugged her arms to her chest tightly, trying for warmth. "Because medically speaking there's very little good I can do." Compared to what she wanted to do, anyway.

Rick stared at her uncomprehendingly. "You helped Mrs. Orlansky, didn't you? You got rid of Clementine's lice and stitched up her foot. You've done physicals for the mine workers, and treated a handful of others."

"Someone else—someone who didn't have a lawsuit pending against him—could do a lot more."

To her relief, he didn't bother to argue what they both knew to be true. "The people here will accept you across-the-board. You just have to give them a chance."

Maybe, Hilary thought, and maybe not.

"I was hoping you'd stay—" he went on persuasively. "Especially after tonight, when I saw how well you were beginning to blend in."

Now it was her turn to stare at him in disbelief. She felt warmed by his praise, alarmed by his expectations, which were so much more than she could ever give. "You know what they say about falling off a horse, that you've got to get back on as soon as possible or you'll never be able to ride again. Well, the same principle applies here. Rick, I need to go back, to prove to myself I can work there. Otherwise, I'll always have doubts. I'll always wonder if I could've cut it there, if only I'd tried one more time. I'm not a quitter. I can't let my career end there in embarrassment and shame."

After a moment, he turned his glance away. "Sorry," he said, his jaw rigid. "I should have realized that was the way it is." He moved stoically past her, being careful not to touch her or invade her physical space. "On second thought, I think I'll pass on the coffee. I've really got to get home, help Mom and Kenny clean up the after-party mess."

She knew a brush-off when she heard one. She also knew that it was best, for both of them, that they maintain their distance from one another emotionally, physically. So why did she feel so let down?

Chapter Seven

The phone rang at six the next morning. Hilary yawned and reached for it, dragging the receiver into bed with her.

"H'lo." She pushed back the covers and sat up.

"Hilary?" Rick croaked hoarsely on the other end of the line. "Sorry to call so early, but I thought I'd let you know I'm sick. I woke up this morning with some sort of flu bug. There's no way I can go into the clinic today, and we're booked solid."

Instantly concerned, she sat up all the way. "Do you want me to call people and start canceling?"

There was a rustling sound as Rick covered the receiver, the wrenching sound of him coughing. "No, I want you to see my patients."

Under normal circumstances, his was a perfectly reasonable request, but these circumstances weren't normal and they both knew it. "I—I don't know..." she warned.

He covered the phone again and coughed even harder. When he spoke again, he was so hoarse she could barely understand him. "Just let them know I'm sick and I'll be out for several days. Please, Hil."

"All right," she conceded. "I'll see as many of your patients as I can."

"Thanks." He heaved a sigh of relief. If he needed his days out, he needed her as backup.

Hilary pictured him sick and alone in his bed. The image wasn't as clinical as she would have liked. Shaking off her hopelessly inappropriate thoughts, she said kindly, "Is there anything I can do for you?" Heaven knew he had done enough for her.

"No." His refusal was firm.

"Rick—"

"All I need is rest, and I'll be fine..." he stressed defiantly.

Wasn't that just like a man, she thought, feeling both exasperated and amused. They thought all they had to do was act macho and ignore their symptoms and then whatever ailed them would magically go away. On the other hand, Rick was a physician. He ought to know if he had something that needed another physician's attention.

"...I'm going to take my phone off the hook the rest of the morning, see if I can't go back to sleep."

Hilary knew sleep would do him more good than anything. But if he didn't get better and soon, she would go over and take a look at him herself. Deciding she was overreacting, she pushed her worrisome thoughts aside. "All right. Take it easy and give me a call if you need anything."

"Will do. And thanks, Hil," he said softly. "I appreciate your helping me out more than you know." The receiver clicked as he hung up the phone.

Hilary sat for a moment, her bare legs dangling over the side of the bed. Well, this day was certainly going to be different. Thinking of the work ahead of her, she began to smile. Imbued with a sense of purpose for the first time in weeks, she got up and headed for the shower.

"I DON'T WANT TO SEE no Dr. Morgan. I want to see Dr. Burnett."

That complaint was echoed time and again over the next few days. She had a few of her own patients. But some of Rick's patients with minor complaints, finding out Hilary was the only choice for medical care, turned right back around and vowed they would wait until Rick came back, no matter how long it took. Others with more pressing complaints—like high fevers or killer stomach cramps or miserable itching rashes—reluctantly saw Hilary.

By the third day of Rick's absence, word had gotten out that she wasn't the quack Emma Schwartz touted her to be, and by day's end Hilary realized with satisfaction that she had seen and treated over thirty-five patients. Not bad, she thought, for her first real week of work since the news about the malpractice suit had gotten out. Not bad, at all.

She was, however, very worried about Rick. "Are you sure it's the flu?" Hilary asked Becca late Thursday afternoon. She knew Becca's husband Will had been over to see Rick Monday, to ensure he was okay.

Becca nodded. "Sure. Why?"

Hilary frowned, unable to shake the nagging feeling that Rick was in danger of some sort. Or at the very least, that he needed to be seen again. "Usually simple viruses run their course in 24 to 48 hours. Since he's not back at work by now, maybe he's getting a secondary infection of some sort."

"Oh, I'm sure Rick would have called Will if he suspected that were the case. Besides, I talked to him this morning. He said he was starting to get better."

Just starting? After four days, now? That didn't sound good, at all. Hilary slipped the stethoscope from around her neck and put it in the black leather bag she used for house calls. "Rick's no slouch. If he were even halfway well, I know he'd be back into work by now, trying to lend a hand." She frowned again, more worried than ever.

"I'm sure that'd be the case, if you weren't here," Becca said carefully, slipping off her own starched white lab coat. She smiled with confidence. "But you are here, so...he knows he can take the time off he needs to get well. Besides, I'm sure he doesn't want to infect any of his patients with what he has."

"I guess you're right," Hilary said slowly. Maybe she was overreacting here. Nonetheless, the thought of Rick suffering with any malady at all disturbed her more than she wanted to admit.

"By the way," Becca said, changing the subject as she locked up the medicine cabinet and prepared to go home. "I saw Mrs. Orlansky this morning. Apparently, she's still having some trouble keeping the supply of glucose to the blood steady."

"Is she keeping to her diet, taking her injections at the times she's supposed to?"

"Yes, but she says she doesn't have the energy she used to have—before she started taking insulin. Personally, I think she is just depressed about having to take insulin for the rest of her life, and that once she adjusts to the idea of it she'll be okay."

"Did you check her blood and urine when you were out there?"

"Yes, both were right on target, which tells me the medication and diet combined is working."

"Well, I'll stop by and look in on her tomorrow morning, before I come in to the office."

"I'm sure that'll make her feel better," Becca said. "She always perks up when you're around."

Hilary grinned. "Only because she has someone to complain to."

Becca laughed. "What are doctors for?"

"Did you look in on Clementine Morris today?" Hilary asked. Becca nodded. "How's her sprained ankle?"

Becca frowned. "Not healing as fast as it might. Daisy said she's having a hard time keeping Clementine off it. Seems every time she turns around Clementine is up to mischief."

Hilary rolled her eyes. "Sounds like Clem."

"I know. I had a talk with her about it, like I'd have with one of my own kids."

"And? Did it do any good?"

"Doubtful."

Hilary smiled again. Clementine wasn't very good at following orders, especially when not doing so got her even more attention from the womenfolk around her. "When Rick gets back and things get a little less crazy around here, I'll drive over and look in on her, too."

"I'm sure she'd like that." Becca grabbed her purse. "I've got to get home and see what my three daring chefs have prepared for our dinner this evening."

Hilary locked up, and medical bag in hand, walked out to the parking lot with her. "Your kids are cooking?" She wondered what it would be like to have three teenagers of her own. Becca and Will's kids always sounded so lively, fun-loving.

"Every night Will and I work, since summer began. Some of their experiments have been . . . well, fascinating."

"Edible?"

"Not always but, bless them, they're trying. At least they all know how to sauté, broil and bake now." Becca got into her car, which had been left unlocked, the windows open.

"That's a start." Hilary said, as she paused to unlock her old pickup and roll down the window before getting in. Turning back to Becca, she turned and spoke through the open window, "You know, I think I'll look in on Rick before I go home tonight. I'm worried about him."

Becca rooted through her purse, hunting for her car keys. "I've known Rick a long time. I'm sure he'll be fine," she reassured, not looking up. "Otherwise, he would've called."

Hilary knew that was probably so. So why was she so worried?

Try as she might, Hilary couldn't put her worry out of her mind, so after Becca drove off she started her truck and headed out to Rick's place anyway. On his front door, a sign had been taped.

Napping. Please don't disturb. Thanks for your concern, I'll be well soon.

Rick

Hilary grinned. So she wasn't the only person who had been here, inquiring about his health. She debated a minute, wondering if she should disturb him.

Deciding finally for her own peace of mind that she at least needed to see how he was doing before she left and make sure he didn't need medical aid of any kind, she rang the bell. And then rang it again.

A few minutes later, Rick opened the door. She had to agree she had never seen him look worse. He was unshaven, his hair all rumpled. Although it was six in the evening he was still in his navy-blue pajama bottoms, with a matching cotton robe pulled on over his bare chest. "Hilary." He paused. "Uh—hi."

The depth of his surprise made her smile. She lifted her medical bag slightly. "I came to see how you were."

The beginnings of an embarrassed flush spread from his neck to his face. "That's sweet, but you really shouldn't have bothered. I'm fine."

He wasn't as steady as he wanted her to believe. In fact, he seemed to be having trouble standing, she noted with alarm. Whether Rick knew it or not, he needed a professional opinion—other than his own. "I really think I should look at you—"

"Hilary—"

"It's either me or have Will drive all the way out here again. Take your pick."

Rick grumbled something she was just as glad not to hear and made his way unsteadily back to the sofa. He sat down heavily. She opened up her bag and extracted a thermometer. "When did the symptoms start?"

"Monday morning."

"And? What did they include?"

Like most doctors, he was a terrible patient—impatient, grumpy, acting as if this should happen to anyone save him, as if he, because of his profession, should somehow be immune from all physical ailments and similar indignities in life. Dropping his eyes, he answered her question tersely, barely moving his jaw, "I think we went over this before, Hil. I had a fever. Cough. Fatigue. General flu symptoms."

"That's it? No sore throat?"

He shrugged. "What can I tell you, it was a mild bug?"

"And yet enough to knock you out for four days, if you count today."

"I'll be back at work tomorrow," he said defensively.

Not if he was still that flushed, he wouldn't. Using her best bedside manner on him, she said gently, "Wait till I check you before you decide that."

"I'm telling you it isn't—"

Hilary stuck the thermometer under his tongue.

He took it right back out, "—necessary."

She raised her brows and spoke as if counseling an errant schoolboy. "Behave."

Rick swore. With a beleaguered sigh, he stuck the thermometer back under his tongue. On impulse, she touched a hand to his cheek. He felt very warm. "What was your temperature this morning?"

"Ninety-nine something."

"Have you taken it since then?"

He shook his head negatively. Getting out her stethoscope, she said, "Let's have a listen to your chest."

Looking pained, he sat back. Although she'd done this literally hundreds of times, it felt odd pushing the robe back from his shoulders. Odder still, moving the stethoscope first over the firmly muscled chest, through the swirls of wheat-gold hair, and then over his back. She was relieved but not surprised to find his heart and lungs were fine. She ran a hand over his collarbone, beneath his jaw, checking for swollen glands, then looked at his ears, nose and throat.

"See? I'm fine." Looking more irritated and grouchy than ever, he pulled his robe back up over his shoulders.

Slowly Hilary replaced her equipment in her bag. "When was the last time you had a look at your throat, big guy?"

"Monday. Why?"

"You've got a hell of an infection there."

"Are you serious?"

"Quite. And your temp's up, too. One hundred and two point eight." She handed him the thermometer so he could read it himself. "Don't tell me you didn't notice?"

He gestured helplessly. "I thought it was just hot in here. I haven't had the air conditioner on."

"And your throat?"

He sighed. "Believe it or not, it doesn't hurt that much. I have had a bear of a headache, though." He paused. "What are you going to do?"

"What do you think?" she said, reaching into her bag for a long cotton swab. "I'm going to take a throat culture and give you a shot. Are you allergic to penicillin?"

"No. Strep, huh?"

"Looks like it," she said, taking the culture she planned to run back to the clinic lab. Although she had no doubt from the beefy red look of his throat and the red dots peppering the roof of his mouth that strepococcal bacterium was present. "As it happens, there's been a lot of it around the last week."

"No kidding?"

"No kidding." She gave him a shot, then asked if he had any penicillin around the house. He did, so there was no need for her to write out a prescription. She reminded him of the dosage he needed to take. "Five days if your lab test turns up negative, ten if it's positive, which I'm betting it will be."

He nodded his understanding. "How are things at the clinic?" he said, as she put her stethoscope back in her bag.

Sensing he wanted her to stay and talk for a few minutes, fill him in on what had happened in his absence, she perched on the arm of the sofa. "Busy."

He leaned back against the cushions. Although physically drained because of his illness, his eyes were bright with interest. "I talked to Becca last night. She said you've been seeing a lot of patients."

She smiled ruefully, thinking how and why that had come about. "They haven't had much choice."

Ignoring her wry tone, he said, "I also heard most of them have been quite impressed."

It was her turn to shrug. "The flu's not all that hard to treat."

His appreciative look deepened. "Maybe not, but you're a damn good doctor and it's about time everyone around here realized it." Their eyes met, held. Without warning, he smiled. "Letting you have the chance to practice again has almost made getting sick worth it."

She grinned, feeling the full brunt of his easygoing charm. "Almost?"

"Yeah, well," He rubbed at his forehead. "Like I said, I've had a bear of a headache the last day or so."

"Strep," they both said in unison, knowing the headache to be a symptom of that malady. Knowing he needed his rest, she rose reluctantly. As much as she hated to leave him, she knew it was best. He wouldn't get any sleep if she was around. "Listen, I've got to go, but call me if your fever isn't down significantly by tomorrow, okay?"

"Okay. And thanks, Hil, for coming by. I'm sorry I was such a bear." With difficulty, he started to rise.

She held up a staying hand. "Stay put. And as for your crankiness—you're sick. You're entitled."

He reached out and caught her hand. "You're great, you know that?" As they regarded one another, the moment strung out tenderly. Slowly he released his grasp on her hand.

Hilary knew, as much as she didn't want to, that she should leave. "Get well, so you can come back to work, Rick." *I've missed seeing you.*

The grooves on either side of his smile deepened. "It's kind of nice, knowing I'm appreciated," he teased.

"Oh, you are," she returned lightly. And not just by his other patients. She'd begun to count on seeing Rick every day, talking to him, laughing with him, and occasionally arguing with him. She hadn't realized how much until he hadn't been there. But she also knew, when she thought about it objectively, that she still didn't want to forge any lasting ties there. When she left she didn't want to have any regrets, and she sensed if she let herself get too close to Rick, she would have plenty.

"I'M FEELING SO GOOD NOW, I don't think I need to take my medicine anymore," Clara Orlansky told Hilary when she arrived to check up on her the following day.

Hilary did a double take. "Wait a minute. I thought you told Becca yesterday you were having some dizzy spells now and again."

"Yes, and I finally figured out why, too. It's because of that medicine I'm taking. That's what's making my blood-sugar levels go all crazy. Up one minute, down the next. If I just stop taking it completely I'll be fine."

"Whoa, Clara. Wait a minute. We talked about this. I explained your condition in depth to you and gave you those pamphlets on diabetes to read. As long as you eat on schedule and take your insulin on schedule you will feel fine, but if you stop," Hilary paused, letting the gravity of her words sink in, "you run the risk of having a seizure or lapsing into a coma. And I'm sure you don't want to risk that."

"You're just trying to scare me," Clara accused, her expression growing stony. She poured Hilary some more iced sassafras tea.

"No, I'm not. I wouldn't do that to you." She paused, wondering uneasily if Clara would be more likely to accept that her condition was lifelong if she heard the news from someone else. "If you'd prefer to talk to another doctor, though, to get a second opinion, I understand."

Clara thumped her walking stick on the floor beside her. "I don't want to talk to no more doctors. I just want to be well again—with no medicine."

"Clara that's never going to happen," Hilary said gently. "This is a lifelong condition. Maybe someday we'll find a cure, but right now all we can do is control it with medication and diet and plenty of rest."

Clara harrumphed. "Done fine without insulin all my life," she muttered. "Don't see why I have to start taking it now. But I can see you won't leave me alone until I do."

"You're right about that much," Hilary said. "I do want you to stay well and I'll do everything in my power to see that you do."

Clara frowned, but said nothing more in response. Apparently she realized this was one battle she wouldn't win, no matter how much she grumbled.

The tiny house seemed stifling in the early morning heat and humidity but Clara, maybe because she was older, didn't seem to feel the heat. Worried about the possibility of Clara getting dehydrated if the temperature got much higher, Hilary looked around, checking to see if there was a way to get better ventilation. "Do you have an electric fan?"

"Did, but it broke."

"Well, I really think you should have one. Either that or stay somewhere a little cooler until this heat wave we're having passes."

"I'll be fine. I always am. If I get too hot, I'll go out on the porch."

There had to be a better way, Hilary thought. "You know, I have several fans. I'd be glad to bring one over for you to borrow."

Clara shook her head. She's as stubborn as a mule, Hilary thought. "Don't need it, and won't use it." As far as she was concerned, Hilary thought, the matter was closed. "Now, how about tasting my new recipe for corn relish for me, like you promised you would when you come in. . . ."

Hilary stayed another half hour. She went to the Morris trailer, where Daisy was still watching over Clementine. To her satisfaction and delight, she noticed much of the junk had been cleared from Wilbur's yard. She commented to Daisy on it. "Kenny and I took all the papers and old cans and glass we could find to the recycling center. We're saving every penny we can get, trying to get as much money in the bank as possible before school starts in the fall."

"Well, it looks a lot nicer around here," Hilary said, pleased Daisy was acting so responsibly.

"My daddy don't think so," Clementine piped up, eager for attention, as always. She climbed up on the sofa next to Daisy and stuck her injured foot out for examination. "He liked things the way they was."

Daisy laced an arm around the little girl's shoulders and pretended to bop Clementine on the head. "Shut up, silly," she teased with genuine love in her voice. "He let us do it, didn't he?"

"You shut up," Clementine teased back, grabbing Daisy around the middle and holding on tight. She buried her head in Daisy's shoulder. "Now you can't ever leave me," she said.

Daisy grinned and kissed her little cousin soundly on the top of the head. "Want to bet? Just wait till my knight comes to take me away."

Hilary knelt on the floor in front of the sofa. "How are the wedding plans going?" Hilary asked, as she unwrapped the elastic bandage from around Clementine's ankle. As she had suspected, it was still bruised and swollen, though not quite as much as before.

"Great," Daisy said. "I got my dress and so did Clem. Alva and my mom are sewing them together."

"They're gorgeous," Clementine drawled, still hugging Daisy with all her might.

"And we're going to be gorgeous," Daisy said.

"Well, young lady," Hilary said, as she rewrapped Clementine's ankle. "Your ankle is getting better."

Clementine made a face. "It still hurts sometimes."

"Only when you jump around on it like you know you're not supposed to," Daisy interjected.

Hilary smiled. Clementine's brows drew together in an angry scowl. "I hate sitting still!"

"Tell me about it," Daisy moaned.

Amused by the repartee between the two girls, Hilary grinned and repeated her instructions on how to care for the sprained ankle. Her business there finished, Hilary stood and prepared to go. "You two take care, and Clementine," she warned, "be careful!"

Clementine giggled and rolled her eyes, but made no comment either way as Hilary said goodbye to Daisy and slipped out the door.

The heat wave they were having didn't abate over the course of the week. Nor did the flu epidemic in the area. When Rick returned to work a few days later, he had all he could do to handle the patients waiting to see him, while Hilary took the overflow and handled house calls. Late Tuesday afternoon, Hilary estimated the temperature to be around one hundred and the humidity roughly the same. The air was so still and hot she felt as if she would suffocate.

Walking wearily into the clinic she was dismayed to find that, despite the window air conditioner, the interior wasn't much cooler. Two patients were waiting to see her, and she had several phone calls to return. Rick was equally busy. By the time everyone left, she was ready to collapse. She walked back out into the waiting room to take a look at the air conditioner. Rick was already there, staring at the humming machine. Although he was still on oral antibiotics, he had completely recovered from his illness. *And a good thing, too,* Hilary thought. She didn't think she could've handled the work load alone. And that made her wonder how he had ever managed before she signed on to help.

"I don't think this air conditioner is working," he said with a frown.

"I don't think so, either." She collapsed into a vinyl waiting-room chair with a groan and promptly stuck to it. "What do we have to do to get it fixed?"

Rick grimaced. "It's hard enough to get a repairman this far out under normal conditions. Ten to one in this heat, it'll be days before we see anyone."

And by then, Hilary thought, the heat wave would have passed. Her own mood sank even lower. Rick, though, didn't seem affected by the broken machinery. Rather, he had taken it in stride and was now contemplating the window unit in a perplexed, engaged manner.

Unbuttoning the first three buttons of his short-sleeved sport shirt, he strode back into his office. "I know I had an instruction booklet around here somewhere."

Too hot to sit still, Hilary got up, too. She followed him back into the rear of the clinic. While he rooted around in his desk, then his file cabinets, she pulled an icy soda from the refrigerator in the coffee room in the back, as well as several ice cubes. She might not be able to cool off, but at least she could quench her thirst.

Rick strode past, waving the booklet. "Found it!" he said victoriously.

Curious as to what he would do, Hilary followed him back to the air conditioner. She slumped in a chair next to him. Opening the soda can, she took a generous swig of the icy liquid, and then another and another.

For several minutes she watched in mute admiration as he consulted the diagrams in the booklet. He was so sure of himself, she thought admiringly. He never appeared to suffer from any self-doubt or anxiety about his own ability—even when working in unfamiliar territory, as he was now.

She wished she had some of his confidence.

Rick turned off the unit and then unplugged it. "I think it's the condenser that's gone bad. If so, we're going to have to take it in."

Her mind focused on the "we" in his sentence and wouldn't let it go. It sounded right, for him to be talking about them that way. And yet there was nothing in his attitude that was anything but businesslike. "Take the air conditioner in where?" she asked, still feeling unutterably lazy.

Rick unscrewed the back cover of the air conditioner, anxious to get a look inside. He slanted her a glance and gave her a smile that made her feel even warmer. "Into Lexington, if we want it fixed right away—and I do. It's been absolutely miserable here, today, and it was even worse when the waiting room was filled to overflowing with patients. The air was so close you could barely breathe."

It had never, ever been this hot and humid in Boston, Hilary thought, absorbed in watching Rick work with the practiced ease of a man used to fixing anything and everything that went wrong in his life. Thank heaven Rick had the kind of character that enabled him to take life's little snarls in stride. Working here would have been utterly miserable if he hadn't reacted so graciously.

Hilary fanned herself with her open palm. "What I wouldn't give to be in central-air right now," she said. Although she was being of absolutely no help to Rick, she was delaying going home because she knew from experience it was probably even hotter there.

"Me, too," Rick said.

"That's right. Your house doesn't have it, either," she murmured, feeling suddenly remarkably content to be there alone with him after-hours. She was getting used to having him around. She liked working alongside him, now that she was seeing her share of patients, too.

Rick studied the interior of the air conditioner. It didn't take him long to find the damaged condenser. "Here's our problem."

"So now what?"

"I screw the panel back on and with your help load it into the back of my truck." He glanced at his watch. "We've got time to make it into Lexington tonight. The department store where I bought it is open until nine. If we deliver it to their service department, it might be ready to pick up in another day or so."

"And if we wait for them to come out?"

"It'd probably be at least another week before they got out here to pick it up and take it back to the store."

"Well, let's go, then," Hilary said.

It was only after they'd started for Lexington that she thought to question why she was going along with him. She could have refused at any point to go into the city with him. But she hadn't. She supposed it was because she enjoyed his company, and because she had missed him those four days he had been sick.

"Want to stop and have dinner before or after we drop off the air conditioner?"

"After," Hilary said. She fanned herself lightly. "I'm still too hot to eat." Although the breeze blowing in his open windows helped, her blouse was still sticking uncomfortably to her.

"Me, too."

They passed a Holiday Inn. Hilary could see the Olympic-sized pool shimmering in the evening sunlight. "There aren't any swimming pools out by us, are there?" She certainly hadn't seen any, and knew she would have remembered if she had.

"No," he answered her politely, "but there's a place not too far from my house—a swimming hole where you can go swimming."

"You mean in a creek?" Hilary asked, appalled.

"Yes." He gave her an appreciative glance, then chuckled, soft and low. Still grinning, he said, "I take it by the look on your face you've never gone swimming in a creek before."

Hilary shuddered, unable to even imagine it. "No."

Again, he laughed softly as his hands comfortably encircled the wheel. "What are you afraid of?"

Did he even have to ask? "Snakes. Tadpoles. Anything living that might rub up against me."

His grin broadened and he shook his head in mute reproof. "You don't know what you're missing."

"Oh, I think I do." And it was nothing she couldn't live without.

His eyes dancing merrily, he tempted casually, "That cool water can feel awfully good on days like this."

Hilary looked straight ahead, not about to be talked into anything so uncivilized, not even by him. "Cool, muddy water, you mean."

He merely looked at her and didn't reply. She couldn't tell what he was thinking. She only knew a shiver ghosted over her skin. They didn't talk again until they reached the mall where the department store was located. Rick backed his truck up to the service entrance while Hilary went to get a store clerk to help them. Half an hour later, they were all set. "Hopefully the air conditioner will be fixed by Monday evening, like they promised," Rick told her happily after completing the last of the paperwork.

"Maybe the warm front will disappear by the time the weekend is over and we have to go back to work," Hilary hoped.

Rick's eyes were dancing with laughter as he shook his head, no. "Sorry, not much chance of that. I listened to the weather report this morning on the way to work. They said it will be Wednesday, at the earliest, before we get any relief."

Hilary groaned, not ready to go back to that steam bath she currently called home. "Let's find some place air-conditioned for dinner."

He took her elbow. "There's a steak place at the other end of the shopping mall."

The touch of his hand cupping her elbow was so familiar. Exciting, in a strange forbidden way.

He paused. "What's the matter?"

He'd read her expression so easily. Hilary wasn't used to having someone that tuned in to her private thoughts. "Nothing." She shook off her response to him. For a moment, it just felt like a date, but that was silly. Surely he didn't need or want close ties with her. He knew she planned to leave soon. She was going back to Boston, to the type of work she'd been trained for. And this was nothing more than a meal shared with a colleague.

Right now they could be friends, pals, but that was all. Fortunately for her, that was all he seemed to want.

Chapter Eight

The following day Hilary got ready to go to the fair. Having finished braiding her hair, Hilary took a look in the mirror. In knee-length khaki walking shorts and a yellow cotton camp shirt, she still looked the native Bostonian she was.

Unexpectedly a wave of homesickness washed over her. She longed for the panorama of restaurants and musical entertainment to choose from, the excitement of a Celtics or Red Sox game. She longed to be back in the city with the concrete underneath her feet. She felt secure there. She knew what to expect.

She didn't know what it would be like to be a judge at the county fair. Then again, how difficult could it be? All she had to do was taste and rate each entry. Hilary groaned out loud, thinking about the prospect. The women knew how to cook—it was one of their main pleasures in life. The task ahead of her would be among the hardest she'd ever tackled in her life.

Happily, Alva was there to greet her and pin a blue ribbon badge on her shirt. Canned goods, desserts and main dishes were lined up on folding tables. "Daisy was supposed to enter her home-baked apple pie, but she hasn't shown up yet," Alva fretted. She checked the time. "If she doesn't get here soon, she'll miss out on the chance to compete."

"Where's Kenny?"

"He had to work today."

"I'm sorry he's going to miss the fair," Hilary said.

Alva nodded, a troubled look on her face.

"Don't tell me you're going to judge," Emma Schwartz said, as Hilary made her way down the line, tasting various homemade preserves on tiny pieces of white bread.

Hilary's cheeks warmed under Emma's provoking stare. Hearing the beginnings of an unpleasant scene, Rick made his way to her side. "Hi, Emma," he said pleasantly. He draped an arm casually over Hilary's shoulders. He was so close to her, their sides were touching. "I see you entered something in almost every category."

Emma nodded. She glanced at Hilary unhappily before looking back at Rick again. "I'm trying to promote the use of recipes that don't have artificial additives or preservatives."

Was it Hilary's imagination, or did Emma look as
if she was retaining water again? She knew it was none
of her business...Emma wasn't her patient...or even
her friend, and yet... Seeing potential trouble for the
young woman from a medical standpoint, it was difficult to stand idly by and do and say nothing.

"Great." Rick smiled at Emma, appreciating her
enthusiasm for the fair, if not her rudeness to his co-
worker. "Hilary? I could use some help on the pies, as
soon as you're done with the jam."

"Ignore Emma," he said when Hilary joined him
seconds later.

If only it were that simple, Hilary thought. Unable
to remain silent, she said, "Is she still seeing an obstetrician in Lexington?"

Rick turned to her, surprised and perplexed. As he
should have been, Hilary thought, since she'd been so
adamant previously about not getting involved with
Emma's care. If only she'd been able to stick to that
resolve.

"Yes." Rick regarded her closely. "What is it?"

*It's not as if I'm actively involved in patient care
here*, she thought defiantly. *Rick probably already
knows what should be done. And even if he doesn't,
Emma's obstetrician in Lexington surely does.* "I just
wondered if she had been advised to go on bed rest."

Rick nodded slowly, still watching her carefully.
"Yes, as a matter of fact. Emma was complaining to
me about that the other day. She also mentioned Dr.

Leiberman would like her to take a leave of absence from her job—"

"But she won't," Hilary finished for him.

"She feels the continuing reforestation efforts are too important. She also confessed she needed to keep busy."

Hilary glanced back at Emma. Even from a distance, she could see the young woman wasn't looking good. Her hands, face and legs were definitely swollen. Her blood pressure was probably elevated, too. If she wasn't feeling well, that could explain her unusually prickly mood. "I don't like it, Rick. Maybe if you were closer to a fully equipped hospital with a neonatal care unit it would be different."

"Dr. Leiberman thinks there's a chance—if she keeps on this way—that she could lose her baby, too," Rick said, frowning. "He asked me to try and talk some sense into her and I've tried, but she won't listen to me, either." He looked at her hopefully. "Maybe if you tried—"

She met his gaze frankly. She wanted to help, but she knew it was an impossible situation. "If it were anyone else...maybe...I could say a few words to her informally. But she doesn't trust or like me, as it is."

"I know you're in a tough situation here," he said sympathetically.

But he also wished it were different, that Hilary could help out; she could tell, by the mixture of wistfulness and disappointment on his face. "Couldn't you try and talk to her again, Rick? Tell her that if she keeps up she could deliver prematurely, that if her blood pressure is too high at the time of delivery, she runs the risk of developing an aneurysm, maybe having a stroke—''

Although Hilary wanted badly to help, she also remembered Dash's warning to her. Emma's was exactly the kind of high-risk case Hilary was supposed to stay away from. Like it or not, she had to honor her promise to Dash, consider her future and keep her distance—no matter how difficult it was to do so.

Rick's mouth thinned unhappily as he confided. "I wish it were that simple. Believe me, I've tried to get her to listen, to take precautions. Dr. Leiberman and I both have. She thinks if she takes it easy, slows down a bit, she'll be fine."

A chill went through Hilary as she realized Rick could be vulnerable to a lawsuit, too. "Rick, I don't want to sound cruel, but...maybe you should drop her as a patient, if she won't follow instructions," she said seriously. She would hate for what happened to her to happen to Rick. "Maybe if you do that, then Emma will finally realize just how serious her situation is. Then if she wakes up to the dangers and starts cooperating, you could take her back on."

Rick shook his head in mute frustration. "Even if I thought that tack would work, I couldn't do it. I work for the county. Anyone who wants medical care at the clinic gets it. Emma knows that, and she also knows where to lodge a complaint if I were to try and shake some sense into her that way. In this case, for the moment anyway, my hands are tied.''

Hilary knew Rick wasn't very concerned about his own fate in this. He just cared about his patient. Once she had felt that way, too. The more idealistic side of her nature still did. The part of her that had been burned, however, made her much more cautious. She wanted him protected from the sort of hardship she had suffered. She knew it would make her sound selfish and hard-hearted, but for his sake she persevered. ''Rick, if something does go wrong, and Emma sues...you could lose everything you've worked for.'' For that reason alone, she worried. She also knew he wouldn't walk away, any more than she was able to stop caring for and about Emma and her baby from a distance. They were patients. And Rick and Hilary were both trained to help.

He considered for a long moment. Finally he met her gaze frankly. ''I still wish you could talk to her yourself, but I understand the reasons why you feel you can't, so I'll talk to her again,'' he said. Excusing himself, he made his way to Emma's side. The conversation they had looked anything but pleasant. Unable to stand being sidelined from obstetrics, and feeling so useless, Hilary turned away completely. When would her life ever be back to normal? she wondered. When would she be able to function as thoroughly and competently and completely as she had been trained to do?

"Hi, Dr. Hilary!" Without warning, Clementine bounded up beside Hilary. "Have you seen Daisy and Kenny? Daisy promised I could have a piece of her apple pie after it was judged!"

Hilary smiled at her little friend, relieved to have found such a pleasant distraction from her problems. "I'm sorry, honey. I haven't seen her."

Clementine's lower lip jutted out. For a moment, she looked as if she was about to cry. Whirling, she turned and headed for Alva. Seconds later, she was demanding plaintively to see her cousin.

Hilary was about to go after her when Rick returned. "Emma refuses to go home now, but she says she'll stay in bed all day tomorrow."

That wasn't enough, Hilary knew. Disturbed by the potential complications and her powerlessness to do anything about the situation, she turned her attention back to the judging. Knowing what was at stake, it was difficult keeping her mind on the task at hand, but somehow she managed. Several hours later, the panel had decided upon winners in all categories.

Exhausted and full, Hilary and Rick handed in their judges' badges. Over the next hour and a half, they roamed all over the attractions, visiting booth after booth. Clementine came back and escorted them to the 4-H exhibits to see her goat. "Daddy got her for me at the beginning of the summer," Clementine said, patting the goat's small gray head.

"Where's your Dad?" Rick asked.

Clementine swung her arms back and forth. "He had to work at the mine. I came with some of my other cousins."

"How come they aren't with you?" Hilary asked. Clementine seemed lonely tonight, isolated.

"They all have 4-H projects, too. One of my cousins made a quilt. Johnny's raising a cow. Pete has two pigs. And Mandy and Delilah are both in the sewing competition, too."

"Sounds like you have one busy family!" Hilary said.

Clementine smiled broadly and puffed out her chest. "My goat is going to win. Just you wait and see."

The announcer stepped up to the microphone. One by one, the winners of the animal competition were called up to the stage. Clementine didn't get a prize. Disappointed, she began to cry.

Hilary sensed it wasn't just the loss of the contest but something more getting the little girl down. She bent down so the two of them were at eye level and took Clementine into her arms. "There, there, honey, it's going to be all right," she soothed. Glancing up at Rick, she saw he looked as concerned as she was.

When the sobs had subsided slightly, Rick touched Clementine's shoulder. "Would you like to go and get some cotton candy?"

Clementine shook her head sadly. "No thank you, Dr. Rick. I think I just want to go home, so Daisy can take care of me."

Rick went off to speak to Clementine's aunt, who had her hands full with her own five children. "Evidently Daisy called her aunt and said she'd changed her mind about attending the fair. She's supposed to meet Clementine at the Morris trailer at five o'clock and keep watch over Clementine until her dad can get home to take over."

"Daisy didn't tell me she wasn't coming," Clementine sniffed, wiping her eyes with one grimy sleeve.

Seeing how hurt Clementine was, Hilary felt her heart go out to her. "I'm sure she meant to," Rick soothed.

Briefly a guilty look crossed his face. Hilary knew what he was thinking—that Daisy and Kenny had changed their plans to attend the fair rather suddenly.

The trailer was eerily silent as Rick parked his truck beside it. He got out. Clementine ran for the door. Seconds later, she came back outside. "Nobody's there," she said, in a trembling voice. She handed Rick an envelope. "But this was here. It has your name on it, too."

"MOM, WILL YOU CALM DOWN?" Rick said half an hour later as he watched her pace back and forth beside the cotton candy booth.

"It's all your fault, you know. If you hadn't been so disapproving of them, he and Daisy never would've felt they had to run off and elope—"

"At least he quit his job at the mine," Rick countered, crossing his arms over his chest.

His mother didn't argue that point, to his relief. He felt guilty enough as it was.

"We've got to find them," she said urgently, looking even more distressed.

"Kenny said in his note they'd be back once they finished their honeymoon."

His mother's light blue eyes were troubled. "What if they don't come back?"

"They will." About that much, Rick was certain. "Daisy's enrolled at Pikeville College for the fall term. She won't give up her tuition scholarship. It means too much to her."

After a moment, his mother broke the silence with a sigh. "I guess you're right." She shook her head wearily, running a hand through her gray-brown hair. "I think I'm going to go home now. I've lost my ability to enjoy the fair."

His feelings of guilt increasing, he watched her walk off. He was hurt and angry at Kenny for eloping, abandoning the wedding plans his mother and Daisy's family had made. But there wasn't much he could do about it now. He hadn't known his disapproval had been so transparent. So glaring.

Hilary came back to join him. "It's all arranged. Clementine is going to spend the night with her cousins, since Daisy is unavailable to baby-sit and Wilbur won't be home from the mine until late."

Rick took her elbow and guided her around the concession stand. He ordered a soda for each of them, watching as Hilary drank gratefully from her cup. "Is she okay?"

This time Hilary was slower to answer. "She's pretty distressed, actually." Her eyes lifted to his, stayed. "She counts on Daisy more than I think any of us realized."

"I never realized how much. Poor kid." He ate his hot dog plain, and ruminated.

Now that darkness had fallen, the fairground had taken on a different glow. The sky was like black velvet and sprinkled with stars. The moon rose high in the sky. He watched as Hilary downed the rest of her sandwich and drained her soda. He felt fenced-in, suddenly restless. He didn't like feeling ineffective, yet lately that was all he'd been. First with Kenny and Daisy, and now Clementine. Not to mention the fact that his mother was mad at him and probably would remain so for some time.

Hilary watched over Clementine from a distance. Although several minutes had passed, she didn't look any happier than she had when she'd first learned of the elopement. "I feel like we should do something for Clementine," Hilary murmured compassionately. "You know, something to break this cycle of accidents and then attention."

"I do, too. Maybe I can have a talk with Wilbur, when things calm down."

"Do you think it'll help?"

Rick shrugged, knowing that about that there really was no predicting. "There's not much else we can do, as outsiders." She looked ready to protest their lack of action. He added, "Besides, you're going to be leaving soon." As much as he hated to admit that to himself, he knew he had to keep it in mind. Because if it weren't for the temporary nature of her stay, he knew he might put their relationship on a more intimate level. But he couldn't do that, not knowing she still had one foot out the door. Realistically, he had to respect her state of mind.

Red stained Hilary's cheeks. "Maybe you're right," she mumbled. "Maybe I am letting myself get too involved."

If Dash has his way, Hilary will be out of here faster than I can blink. "Maybe you can go into town tomorrow, get your mind off your work for a while."

"Maybe," Hilary agreed. But she didn't sound enthused, and Rick was feeling very down.

When he left, he decided it was best for the moment to keep his distance from Hilary.

Chapter Nine

"How long has Stevie been running a fever?" Hilary asked his mother, Mary Lou Pritchart, the following morning. Saturday she had agreed to man the clinic. Rick was making a few house calls. With the flu still going round, they had plenty of people to see.

"Since late last night," the affable young mother replied, looking anxiously over at her six-year-old son. "I guess it was around nine when he told me he didn't feel well. I took his temperature. It was ninety-nine point six. It's been about the same ever since."

Although his fever was still low-grade, it was obvious Stevie was ill by the unusually pale color of his skin. Normally a rambunctious child, he was also far quieter than usual. Since he'd entered the examining room with his mother, he hadn't said a word. Suspecting him to be infected with the same flu bug that had sidelined Rick and countless others in the county the past few weeks, Hilary checked his glands and found them to be swollen. "Any other symptoms?" She looked from Mary Lou to Stevie, asking, "Is your tummy upset? Do you have a headache?"

Stevie shook his head no to both questions. "But my throat hurts when I swallow."

"Let's have a look." Finding both pharynx and tonsils to be red and swollen, Hilary took a throat culture, then stepped across the hall to their small lab to run the test herself.

"Well, the good news is it isn't strep," Hilary told mother and son minutes later. "But I'm going to put you on antibiotics anyway for five days to prevent any secondary bacterial infection from developing while you are ill. In the meantime, you need to stay quiet and out of the sun as long as you're running a fever." She ripped the prescription off the pad and handed it to Mary Lou. "You also need to drink plenty of fluids. He can have juice, soft drinks, milk, whatever he wants. But keep him hydrated," she told Mary Lou.

"I'll take good care of him," Mary Lou said, looking relieved.

"And make sure he gets all of his medicine," Hilary cautioned. "Don't stop giving it to him as soon as his fever goes away."

"I won't."

"'Bye, Doctor Hilary," Stevie said.

Hilary handed him a brightly colored sticker of a cartoon animal saying, "I'm a good patient!" and watched as he proudly peeled off the back and stuck it to the front of his Ghostbusters T-shirt.

"Bye, hon!" she said, patting Stevie on the shoulder. "Feel better!" As she watched him go, she felt a real sense of satisfaction, one she hadn't expected to feel. She had always enjoyed taking care of pregnant women, delivering babies, but caring for whole families, children and their parents and the elderly alike, had its share of satisfactions, too. She was going to miss it when she went back to obstetrics. Maybe almost as much as she would miss seeing Rick. But she also knew the sooner her own situation was resolved, the better. She wanted to put the Jones case behind her and get on with her life, deliver babies again. And keeping that in mind, she picked up the phone to call Dash, to see if there was any news.

He wasn't in, so she left a message with his answering service.

A few more patients trickled in and she had just finished the paperwork on them when the phone rang.

"DR. MORGAN, I'm sorry to bother you on the weekend, but I'm very worried about Clara Orlansky," Sadie Porter said. "I stopped by her place a while ago, and she was nowhere in sight."

"Maybe she went out," Hilary said. "Now that she's been feeling better, she's been doing that more often."

"I know she has, but I don't think that's the case this time. There was peach jam on the stove, doc. It had boiled down to almost nothing. Clara never would have walked out with a pot of jam still cooking on the stove."

Alarm had her on her feet, starting to pace. A day or two without insulin could be fatal to the elderly woman. "And you say you can't find her?" Hilary was already reaching for her car keys.

"I looked everywhere. She isn't in the house. That's why I called you. I know she's diabetic, and that people with her condition sometimes become confused or ill if their blood-sugar level gets too high or too low. Doc, what are we going to do?"

"We're going to find her." *And then pray she's all right*. Her calm voice disguised the anxiety she felt, and Hilary said, "I'll be right over. In the meantime, you stay on the phone. Call everyone you think she might have gone to visit and see what you can dig up."

"Will do, and thanks, doc."

No sooner had Hilary hung up than she dialed Rick's beeper. To her relief, he called a few minutes later. Quickly she told him what had transpired. Sounding as worried as she felt, he agreed to meet her at Clara's.

They arrived within minutes of one another. Hilary crossed quickly to Rick's side. He, too, looked like he had just got out of bed. "Anything?"

"No," he said shortly. Others were pulling up into the yard and piling out of cars. "I think we better search the woods." Rick began dividing everyone up into small groups. "Hilary, you come with me."

She didn't argue. Rick could find his way around any woods blindfolded, while she still sometimes got lost just driving from her house to Alva's.

"She was doing so well," Hilary said as they searched the orchard next to Clara's home.

"I know," Rick said, taking her hand and squeezing it briefly. "Maybe she just got confused."

"Maybe," Hilary thought, as the first nagging doubt crossed her mind. And maybe there was some symptom of this calamity there the last time she had seen Clara, and she just hadn't noticed. The way she hadn't noticed with Mrs. Jones.

Minutes later, Hilary spotted something white down near the bottom of a ravine. A chill of fear sliding down her spine, she tugged on Rick's arm. "Rick, down there," she said in a trembling voice.

"Oh no," he said softly, seeing what she'd found. "Let's go."

The two of them took off at a run. Clara was lying face-down at the bottom of the ravine, one fragile arm flung out from her body.

Praying she was still alive, Hilary gingerly felt for a pulse. It was weak but discernible.

"Whasha doin' ta me?" Clara mumbled drunkenly, trying to fling off Hilary's probing touch. "Jush let me shleep..."

"She's slipping into a diabetic coma," Rick said.

"It looks like she's broken her leg," Hilary said, pointing to the swelling knot above Clara's thigh.

Clara moaned, the pain she felt radiating in her voice.

"You stay with her. I'll run back to get help," Rick said.

He returned minutes later with a quilt, three two-by-fours and several towels, Clara's insulin, a clean white sheet and his medical bag. "There's only one ambulance serving this part of the county and it's on another call, so we're going to have to transport her ourselves," he said.

Hilary felt the first stirrings of panic. It was situations like this she was most afraid of. It reminded her too much of her sister's death, her helplessness, the waiting for the ambulance that never got there in time. Pushing away the awful memories, Hilary sprang into action. "Can't we get another?" she asked, tearing the sheet into seven long pieces and laying them out one by one.

"Only if we're willing to wait at least an hour, and I'm not." Rick carefully began straightening Clara's leg enough to splint it, ignoring her half-conscious moans of pain. "Wilbur Morris is bringing down a makeshift stretcher." Using a stick, he began pushing the strips of cloth under Clara's body at the hollow beneath her knee, her ankle, the small of her back, while Hilary took the insulin kit from his medical bag and prepared an injection.

"How's she doing?" he asked.

Briefly Hilary filled him in on what she'd found in her initial exam of their patient. "There doesn't seem to be any other injury, aside from the broken leg."

"Probably forgot to take her insulin this morning," Rick said.

Hilary nodded.

Working like a well-rehearsed team, Hilary and Rick padded the three boards with towels, then moved one beneath her injured leg and one on either side of it. Quickly they tied the splint in place with knots.

Clara opened her eyes as they finished, and looked around in confusion. "Where am I?" she asked in bewilderment. Her speech was no longer slurred. She winced in pain when she tried to move.

"You had a fall, Clara," Rick said.

"But you're going to be fine," Hilary reassured.

Wilbur Morris and two other neighbors came down the ravine, carrying a twin-sized mattress that would serve as a stretcher. They set it down beside Clara. With Rick and Hilary directing and assisting, four of them moved Clara onto the lumpy mattress. Though they tried to be gentle, the movement brought moans of anguish from the injured woman. Clara was sobbing with pain as they picked her up and began a cautious, time-consuming trek up the treacherously steep ravine.

Hilary was shaking with exhaustion and nerves by the time they reached the station wagon that had been recruited for use as an ambulance.

The owner elected to drive, while Hilary and Rick crouched in the back with Clara. "Where to, doc?"

"Lexington General."

Clara moaned again as the car started up. Hilary reached out and took her hand. It was going to be a long ride.

"YOU OKAY?" Rick asked two hours later, as Hilary stood before the window, looking out at downtown Lexington. The city was so safe. If Clara had been injured nearby it would have been so much easier, so much faster to treat her.

"I'm fine. It's Clara I'm worried about."

He wrapped his arms around her. She leaned into his chest, needing to feel his strength, his warmth. "She should be out of surgery soon," Rick reassured.

She fell silent for a moment, brooding. It wasn't like her to be emotional over a patient. Except for rare cases—as with Dash and his wife—she didn't even know her patients, not personally, anyway, not outside the office. But that had changed when she moved to Kentucky to practice with Rick. There, she knew everyone. And because of that she felt personally involved with patients, so much so that she had tears in her eyes as she looked at Rick. Worse, her voice sounded as shaky and disturbed as her mood. "You realize she could have died, if we hadn't found her when we did."

The flat of his hand moved in soothing, circular fashion over her back. "But she didn't."

Despite the reassurance in his voice, in his touch, the chill in her soul just wouldn't go away. "But she could have died, Rick." She turned toward him, fear making her voice catch and quiver. "If her neighbor hadn't dropped in to check on her, if we hadn't realized she was missing—"

"The jam on the stove would have caught fire. The fire department would have arrived. One way or another we would have figured out what happened and found her in time."

Hilary was silent. Her brain told her he was right. Her heart was still in a panic.

"I know it's been traumatic for you, Hilary. For Clara, too. But it's over. She's going to be all right." Rick's arms tightened around her. As tender as his touch was, it did nothing for the apprehension inside her.

Knowing she was still treacherously close to falling apart, Hilary took a deep, steadying breath and said, "She'll have to be here for weeks." Clara wouldn't like it at all. She loathed the city as much as Hilary had loathed the isolation of the country.

"Maybe even months," Rick agreed. He drew a careful breath and continued to stare out at the city. "Once the leg heals, she'll have to go through physical therapy in the rehabilitation unit, if she wants to walk again, and I'm sure she will."

Hilary was silent. The logical part of her knew she should move away from Rick. She was asking for trouble, leaning against him like this. But he felt so warm, so right, and she was in need of comforting herself.

Giving in to the desire for protection, she rested her cheek against his shoulder, loving the solid feel of him against her face.

"In case I didn't tell you earlier, you were great today," Rick said softly, threading his fingers through her hair. The light, caressing touch of his fingers on her scalp had her tipping her head back to see his face better.

"You were great, too," she said meaning it. The first hint of a smile touched her lips. She was still marveling how well and effortlessly the two of them had worked together. They hadn't even needed to talk about what they were going to do. They'd responded on instinct, his every action complementing hers, and vice versa. She wondered obliquely what it would be like to make love to him, if they would have the same symmetry of thought and motion. If so, the experience would be incredible.

She chided herself for even fantasizing about it, and moved away from him. She thought, but couldn't be sure, she saw a fleeting spark of hurt in his eyes, but it was gone as quickly as it had appeared.

"I think I'll get a cup of coffee," she said, once again a marvel of human efficiency. "Can I get you anything?"

He shook his head negatively and didn't speak for almost a minute. Still watching her with narrowed eyes, he said slowly, "I'm fine, thanks."

Why did she suddenly doubt that?

"YOU GAVE US QUITE A SCARE," Hilary said hours later, leaning over Clara's bed. Reflexively, she checked the IV line running into Clara's arm. It was fine.

Clara smiled groggily at Hilary. "Serves you doctors right," Clara mumbled cantankerously. "Since you're always scaring me."

Rick laughed. He stood beside Hilary, looking no less devoted to the older woman than she felt. "Well put, Clara. What I want to know is how you got out there in the first place. What were you up to?"

Clara was quiet, thinking hard. Finally, she shook her head. "I don't know. The last thing I remember was deciding to make peach preserves."

"You started that, all right," Hilary said. "They were still cooking on the stove when you left the house."

"Land sakes!" Clara said. "It's a wonder I didn't burn my whole house down. I didn't, did I?"

"No. Everything's fine." Hilary and Rick exchanged a look. Knowing it was time, Hilary said, "Did you take your insulin this morning, Clara?"

Clara colored guiltily. "No. I didn't think I needed it."

"Well, that explains how and why you became confused," Hilary said gently. "I hope you won't do that again."

"No. I won't." Clara looked at her solemnly. If Hilary thought Clara needed scolding, she would've done so at that moment, but she knew the woman had already been through enough. After a moment, she said, "I really am glad you're all right."

"My preserves," Clara muttered. "What am I going to do this winter, if I don't get those preserves made? I always have peach preserves, every year. Apple jelly, too. And with the fruit on the trees ripening now..."

"Relax. I'll see your jam is made. And I'll be sure the recipe is tailor-made for your needs." Although she'd never canned anything before, Hilary was sure Alva could tell her everything she needed to know.

"You'd do that for me," Clara asked, tears spilling from her eyes, "after all the trouble I've caused you?"

Hilary smiled down at her and took Clara's hand in hers. She might not want to stay here forever, but as long as she was here, she would become part of the community. "What are friends for?" she asked softly.

"WHEN DID STEVIE'S fever come back?" Hilary asked Mary Lou Pritchart Friday morning.

"In the middle of the night."

Although she knew the facts by heart, Hilary picked up his chart to more thoroughly review the case. "And he finished taking his medicine when?" It should have been Wednesday, she thought.

"He had the last dose of antibiotics Wednesday evening," Mary Lou confirmed. "The fever started approximately twenty-four hours later. And then when I was getting him dressed this morning to bring him in, I noticed this rash." She pointed to the raised red bumps covering him from shoulders to feet.

Hilary already had a good idea what it was—and it wasn't good. Wanting to be sure before she spoke, she ran a quick blood test and found his white count to be high. The second throat culture tested positive. Her worst fears were confirmed. Stevie Pritchart was on his way to being one sick little boy.

Thank goodness he had a mother who'd had the good sense to bring him in immediately, at the first hint of further illness. Otherwise, she realized shakily, the outcome of all this could have been very different. Left untreated, Stevie could've become seriously ill, suffered permanent heart or kidney damage.

Was she responsible? Hilary didn't want to think so. She wanted to believe she had done all she could for him when he had been in before. Certainly his condition had seemed very straightforward, the diagnosis obvious. Inside, she couldn't be sure she hadn't missed something last week. Maybe there had been some sign there...maybe this was like the Jones case...maybe there was something she had missed.

Unfortunately she couldn't turn back the clock, and because she couldn't, now they would never know.

Telling herself to buck up, she pushed aside her guilt and fears and hurried back to the examining room where Stevie and his mother waited.

"Scarlatina!" Mary Lou Pritchart exclaimed, alarmed, when she heard Hilary's diagnosis. "How did he get that? And what is it?"

Concentrating on the full recovery she knew Stevie would make, Hilary said calmly, "It's a mild form of scarlet fever and it's caused by streptococcus bacteria."

Mary Lou's mouth dropped. She stared at Hilary, dumbfounded. "But you said when I had him in last week that he didn't have strep throat!"

She could feel the doubt, not just in the diagnosis but in her ability as well. Mary Lou Pritchart was no longer sure she was competent to care for her beloved son. "That's right," she continued calmly. "The throat culture I ran then was negative, but lab tests aren't infallible—" Humans weren't, either.

"What about the antibiotics he took?" Mary Lou said.

"It takes a full ten days of oral penicillin to wipe out strep. I'm going to start Stevie on that today and I'm also going to give him a shot. The injection alone would wipe out the strep, but just to be on the safe side we're going to do both."

"All right." Mary Lou hesitated, then spoke what was on her mind. "Is . . . is Dr. Rick in today?"

For a moment, Hilary was too stunned to answer. She had expected Mary Lou to be upset about this development. Any mother would have been. But in the past Mary Lou had always seemed to trust Hilary's competence. She was one of the few who had. Unfortunately it seemed that was no longer the case. "Yes," Hilary said, working hard to suppress her hurt, yet knowing it was a patient's right to ask for confirmation whenever the need arose. "Would you feel better getting a second opinion on this?" Most of all, she wanted Mary Lou to be comfortable, to know in her heart Stevie was getting the best of care they could give him.

Mary Lou bit her lip. "Would you mind?"

"Not at all. Let me get him." Telling herself it was ridiculous to feel hurt about this, Hilary exited the examining room as graciously as possible. If she were in Mary Lou's shoes, she would do the very same thing, she told herself firmly.

As Hilary had expected, Rick came to the same conclusion she had about Stevie's illness. Concurring with her diagnosis, he reassured Mary Lou and little

Stevie. Stevie got a shot, a prescription for antibiotics, another sticker and a piece of sugarless gum. He left happily. Hilary was relieved the crisis was over. Nonetheless, deep inside, she couldn't help but feel bad about what had happened, and not surprisingly Rick called her on her self-derisive attitude at closing time.

"Stop being so hard on yourself," he said, the moment the two of them were alone in the clinic. "What happened to you this morning could've happened to anyone."

Her frustration with herself and the situation made her tense. "I ran that throat culture myself. It was negative."

"So maybe, like me, he didn't have strep at that point." Rick stepped into her private office and leaned against the wall.

Hilary met his eyes, needing at that moment to be hard on herself in a way he wouldn't be. "And maybe he did," she countered ruthlessly. "And maybe I missed it."

"Bull. I read his chart. There was nothing when he was in the office last week to indicate strep. His fever was low. He had no other symptoms. You took every precaution. He just got sicker, anyway. The important thing is he's going to be okay."

A warm feeling filled her for this man. "Thanks, Rick."

He came to her, and, arms spread beseechingly, took her shoulders in his hands. "It's the truth," he said gently, holding her as if he wanted to shake some sense into her. His eyes searched her face. "Listen, are you still planning to make jam for Clara?"

"I promised, didn't I?"

His grin widened. "Need an assistant chef?"

"YOU KNOW, you really don't have to help me with this," Hilary said to Rick later that evening as she picked up the empty bushel baskets stacked on Clara's porch and headed for Clara's orchard. "I'm the one who promised to make preserves for her."

He shrugged and kept pace. "I was at loose ends tonight, anyway. Besides, I have no choice. I have to help," Rick continued good-naturedly, taking two of the four baskets from her hands. "How else could I ask for some of the bounty?"

"Ah, I see. A secret agenda. You want some preserves of your own to keep."

"A jar or two. I don't think Clara will mind. Course I'll ask her first."

She grinned, liking the way the sunlight brought out the golden highlights in his hair. The way he could get her mind off her troubles. "You plan ahead," she noted, approving.

He grinned at her mischievously. "Always."

The trees were low and filled with fruit. By unspoken agreement, Hilary concentrated on the lower branches, while Rick picked on the tops of the apple and peach trees. By the time night had fallen, they had four bushel baskets, two each of apples and peaches.

Rick glanced at his watch and frowned. The waning heat had left his face bathed in sweat. She knew she was equally grubby, yet somehow it didn't lessen her yearning for him, or in any way diffuse the memory of the way he had held her at the hospital Sunday afternoon.

Rick took a bandanna out of his back pocket and handed it to her. Soft and rumpled, it smelled of fabric softener and soap. She wiped her face, then handed it over to him, watching in fascination as he did the same.

They each picked up one basket and started for his truck. "It'd probably be better if we wait to get started on the jam until tomorrow night. We could do it at my house. I have a larger kitchen."

She fell into step beside him. "All right." As much as Hilary hated to admit it, she was a little tired. "Clara said to use the mason jars she has in her back room. They'll need to be sterilized and we'll need to get some more jar lids from the store."

"No problem. I can do that on my lunch hour tomorrow," Rick said.

They went back for the other baskets, then parted company. Not surprisingly, news of their jam-making spread. Nearly every patient Hilary saw at the clinic Saturday morning commented on her willingness to help out a neighbor. Unfortunately news of Stevie's scarlatina had also spread. People were still coming to see her, but they looked at her with a new wariness. She sensed the lack of trust and hoped it would fade.

"I'm beginning to feel I should have both saint and sinner affixed to my name," she told Rick drily, later that night. "People love me for what I did for Clara, and they mistrust me because of Stevie."

"The hoopla over Stevie will pass," Rick said firmly. "As for what you did for Clara—well, people are surprised, that's all. When you first came to Crossings, you didn't want help of any kind. Not with your house or anything. They didn't expect to see you so ready to lend a hand to someone in need."

Hilary paused. As discomfiting as it was to admit, Rick was right. She had been standoffish when she had first arrived in Kentucky. Used to the barriers city people put up to insulate themselves from the constant intrusion of others into their physical space. She hadn't understood or appreciated the close-knit community spirit she'd found here. Rather, she had found it a barrier to her acceptance as a doctor.

Hilary pitted another peach. "I guess people are starting to accept me," she said, amazed at the way they were able to work side by side, never getting in one another's way. He hadn't touched her, yet she remained aware of him in a surprisingly sensual way.

Rick grinned, looking not at all surprised by the way the community had latched onto her. "I always knew it would happen," he said simply. "Of course, you've more than proven yourself worthy of that respect."

"What do you mean?"

He looked so calm and capable standing next to her, peeling peaches. So much so that she wondered if there was anything he couldn't do.

"You're a good doctor. A caring physician. They appreciate that."

"I try." Even when she didn't feel she succeeded, she always tried.

They continued to work companionably. When all the peaches had been made into jam, the lids sealed tight, the dishes done, Hilary collapsed on his sofa. "Darn, but that's hard work," she moaned, feeling utterly exhausted. She would never again take for granted anything she bought in a jar or a can.

Rick laughed as he brought in a tray bearing lemonade and a plate of home-baked gingersnaps a patient had brought into the clinic in lieu of cash payment that day. "That mean you're changing your mind about the apples?"

"Not on your life. I'm looking forward to using some of this jam on my toast, too."

Rick grinned. He sank down beside her and flipped on the television, bypassing a rerun of *Terms of Endearment* for the Reds/Astros game. Hilary sighed and bit into a gingersnap. The spicy flavor melted on her tongue. The country cooking was another thing she was beginning to appreciate.

As for Rick's choice of television programs...his taste left a lot to be desired.

"ALL DONE," Rick said early the next evening.

"Amazing," Hilary said. "Four bushels of fruit, and all we got out of it were twenty-four pint jars of preserves."

"It cooks down a lot, doesn't it?"

"I'll say." Hilary yawned and stretched, using both her hands to massage her aching back. "I had no idea how much was involved in making jam."

"Clara appreciates it, though."

Wordlessly, he turned her around and began massaging the tight flesh between her shoulder blades. He worked his way down slowly, his magic fingers on either side of her spine, until he'd reached the tense aching region just above her waist.

"I was glad to help out," Hilary said, a bit breathlessly, as she gave in to the soothing massage of his hands. Darn, but he knew how to touch a woman, she thought. Just how and where and how forcefully to rub.

The tension left her body as if by magic. Satisfied with her relaxed state, he picked up a dish towel and went back to drying some of the dishes they'd used to cook the apples. Feeling as if her body was made of putty, Hilary went back to washing the dishes that were left in his sink.

Needing to talk about something mundane, anything to get her mind off his soothing touch, Hilary said, "It's neat, the way the whole community has rallied round Clara, too. Your mom said they're taking shifts, going in to the hospital in Lexington to visit her."

"That's the way it is around here," Rick said. "When someone is sick or in need, everyone else pitches in to help out. That's one of the reasons I came back here to live."

"And the others?" She found she was holding her breath as she waited for him to answer.

"I love the mountains, the beautiful countryside. My family and friends are here. It's just home to me and always will be."

"And you've never wanted anything else?" Hilary asked, a little disappointed when he nodded, admitting that this was true.

"No. I want to know my patients, their families. I want them to know me."

"You could have that in the city, if you had your own private family practice."

"True, but I wouldn't be needed as much. And that's important to me, too."

Hilary had to admit that was the seductive part of being a physician, feeling really important to your patients. But there was a downside, too. The lack of equipment, no emergency room nearby, the frustration of knowing what to do but not having the equipment to do it with. Not to mention the fear of falling behind in modern medical practice because you were so far out in the sticks.

"Thinking of staying on?" Rick asked.

Hilary wished, to make him feel better, that she could say that was true. But she knew it wasn't and probably never would be. "No," she said softly. "When my difficulties are over, I know I'll go back." The difference was, she now wished Rick would go with her.

He looked at her with thinly veiled disappointment. And this time, when they were finished and Hilary started to go home, he made no effort to stop her. No invitation to stay for cookies and lemonade was issued. Hilary knew it was for the best. She couldn't afford to get too close to him or vice versa, but the disappointment she felt over his renewed distance just wouldn't go away.

Chapter Ten

"This is the third time this week you've been in my clinic, Clementine," Hilary told her small patient Wednesday morning. All were minor reasons. Monday, it had been a skin rash due to a romp in poison ivy. Tuesday, it had been a stubbed toe. Today, a sprained wrist.

Clementine had been staying with her aunt while her father worked, since her cousin Daisy had run off with Kenny, and her aunt and uncle lived close to town, so it was no problem for her to come into the clinic. But Hilary knew from the expression on her aunt's face when she'd brought Clementine into the office, that the daily visits to the clinic were beginning to wear thin.

"I know, but I don't mind," Clementine reported happily, swinging her legs back and forth while Hilary wrapped her wrist in an elastic bandage. "I like seeing you, Dr. Hilary."

Hilary smiled at the genuine expression of affection. "I like seeing you, too." Clementine had a way of brightening up her days, while simultaneously showing her what she had missed by not having children thus far in her life.

Finished, she sat back on her stool and looked up at her patient. With her hair clean and braided, her clothes washed and mended, Clementine looked pretty enough to grace the pages of a Sears catalog.

"But you know," Hilary continued easily, "you don't have to be sick or hurt for us to see one another."

"I don't?" Clementine seemed puzzled.

"No. We could get together and do something, that is if your daddy approved."

"Oh, he would!" Clementine hopped off the table, her discomfort of moments before all but forgotten in the excitement. "What could we do?"

"Well... how about see a movie. I heard there's a new Disney flick out that's supposed to be great!"

"Really? We could go see a movie? In a real theater? I've never been to a movie. I've seen 'em on TV, but... I've never been to a real movie theater."

Incredible, Hilary thought, amazed at the cultural deprivation of some of the children she encountered. She'd seen movies for as long as she could remember. In fact, weekend sojourns to the local theater had been one of the most enjoyable things she'd ever done.

It was also something she had missed, since living in Crossings. There was no theater there, the closest being over thirty miles away. To see a first-run picture, she would have to drive into Lexington.

"Maybe we could drop by and see Clara, too. I'll have to check with the hospital, but I saw children there before, and I think I can get you in."

"Really, that'd be great!"

"Let me call your dad first, though. I have to ask him if it's okay." In retrospect, Hilary realized she had probably made a mistake in not doing so in the first place. Of course, she hadn't had much experience in befriending little children. All her friends in Boston had been roughly her own age, or somehow involved in the medical profession.

Later that afternoon, after the clinic closed for the day, Hilary phoned Wilbur Morris. To her relief, he approved of her idea. "Clementine's been missing Daisy a lot. It'll do her good to be out with a pretty lady like yourself. You sure it's not too much trouble, though?" he persisted. "I don't want Clementine making a nuisance of herself or wearing out her welcome, 'specially since you've been so good to her, taking care of her at the clinic, and all."

"No trouble at all, Mr. Morris. I'm looking forward to the opportunity." They set a date and time, for the following Saturday morning, and then Hilary hung up.

She turned to discover Rick lounging in the doorway. He frowned at her. "Do you think that's a good idea, letting Clementine start to depend on you?"

The implied criticism in his look stung. "It's only one movie, Rick."

"To you, maybe. To her it's the whole world." He straightened and came toward her. "I don't mean to offend you. I know your heart's in the right place. But Clementine is one lonely little girl. Daisy's been babysitting her ever since her mother died. She was like a surrogate mother to her. Clementine was upset enough when Daisy announced her plans to get married and go off to college. Not getting to be in Daisy's wedding didn't help any. If you let her down, too, Hilary—"

"I see what you mean," Hilary said slowly, distressed. She looked at him guiltily. She hadn't thought past easing the girl's immediate hurt. Big mistake. It killed her inside to think she might cause the lonely child even more heartbreak than she'd already suffered in her short life. Miserably she asked, "What can I do?" How could she get out of this, without hurting Clementine even more? "Unfortunately it's already been arranged, the details firmed up."

"I don't know." There was no condemnation in his voice, but she felt it nonetheless. It surprised her to realize she hated disappointing Rick more than Clementine.

The silence between them continued unabated. Hilary searched her mind for a solution. "Maybe...maybe if you or Becca went along, too," Hilary theorized at last. "It would be easier on her, less traumatic when the time came for me to leave."

Already an idea was forming in Hilary's mind. Maybe there wouldn't be one special person Clementine could turn to, but there could be a number of people who would fill the void in her life left by first her mother's, and then Daisy's absence. There was herself, Rick, possibly his mother, and maybe even Becca. All it would take was a little arranging on her part, and she knew it could happen.

"I think I could manage a movie on Saturday with the two of you."

"Great. And don't forget. While we're in Lexington, we're going to drop in on Clara and see how she's doing. I've already cleared it with the hospital."

"I won't forget. In fact, I'll be looking forward to it."

The rest of the week seemed to drag. After spending three days straight with Rick, in the clinic and out, Hilary missed his company when she wasn't with him. That disturbed her, and more than once she was tempted to phone him and invite him over for popcorn and a VCR movie, or something equally mundane. Knowing, however, it would be wrong to count on him that way, not to mention monopolize all his time, she busied herself with other activities. She went to visit his mother, and learned how to quilt. She gave another home-safety class—alone this time—and was pleased to see twenty people attend. She was sorry Emma Schwartz was not among them. Meantime, she continued to work to help collect paper and tin cans for the recycling drive. Her schedule was exhausting, but it left her with little time to brood about her growing feelings for Rick.

Finally Saturday arrived. To say Clem was hyper when they picked her up would have been an understatement. She was practically dancing with joy, and she got no less exuberant as the afternoon wore on. "Are you boyfriend and girlfriend?" she asked them as they left Clara's hospital room.

Hilary felt a blush of embarrassment warm her cheeks. This, she hadn't expected. Nor to her knowledge had she and Rick done or said anything at all to indicate to Clementine that this was the case. "No, we're not," Hilary answered firmly. She slanted a look at Rick and saw he was as discomfited as she by Clementine's question. "What makes you think that?" She turned back to Clementine.

"The way you look at each other all the time, like Daisy and Kenny used to look at each other. You know, kind of sappy or goofy—like you know a secret we don't. Clara noticed, too. She said so when you two went down to the snack bar to buy juice for everyone."

Hilary's cheeks grew warmer and she searched in her purse for a tissue she didn't need. "We're just friends, Clementine."

"Good friends," Rick added, giving Hilary a meaningful look, one that seemed rife with gratitude that she had rescued them from the child's matchmaking as adroitly as she had.

"Oh." Clem looked as disappointed as Hilary sometimes felt. "I was hoping you two would get married so I could still be a flower girl in a wedding."

"I'm sure you'll have other chances to be a flower girl," Hilary reassured her kindly. "Now, on to the movie."

By the time they returned Clementine to her father, she was exhausted. Wilbur Morris thanked them for taking his daughter out and making her Saturday such a special one.

As they got back in the pickup, Hilary felt her own spirits plummet slightly. She'd been having such a good time, despite Clem's embarrassing questions, she was loathe to let the day end. She would have liked to go out to dinner with Rick, or somehow prolong the moment, but he didn't seem similarly inclined. She knew he was acting sensibly, that maintaining some distance between them was for the best, both professionally and personally. There was no sense starting what would inevitably have to end. But the whimsical, romantic side of her couldn't help but feel disappointed.

IT RAINED ALL DAY Sunday and continued during the night. By Monday morning the back roads were muddy and impassable, and Rick knew if it continued, many of the county's narrow one-lane bridges would wash out. Fearing for Hilary's safety, he phoned her house, intending to pick her up and drive her into work. Unfortunately she'd already left by the time he called. He found himself praying she was safe the whole drive to the clinic. His relief was profound when he arrived and found her truck parked in the rain-drenched lot in front of the clinic.

When he stepped in the back door, the first thing he heard was the phone ringing. The second was the sweet, melodic sound of Hilary's voice as she answered it. Rick smiled at the familiar sound, then frowned as he realized who she was talking with.

"Dash, hi," Hilary said, as Rick shook the rain off his yellow slicker and poured himself a cup of coffee.

Hearing the surprise and delight in his temporary partner's voice, Rick felt a stab of jealousy. He knew Dash was nothing more than a friend to Hilary. Dash Barrington was also everything Rick wasn't—sophisticated, prep-school-educated, the kind of guy who not only belonged in the city but reveled in living there. Just talking to him probably reminded Hilary of everything she had given up when she had moved to rural southeastern Kentucky.

Although he tried not to eavesdrop, from his vantage point Rick could hear everything she was saying.

"That's wonderful!" Hilary said. And then more softly, more disappointedly, "Oh...yes, I understand. Alone, that doesn't necessarily prove...yes. I'll wait to hear from you. Thanks."

Rick waited until she hung up the phone, then crossed the hall and went into her office. Wanting to insure they not be overheard by any of the patients beginning to arrive, he shut the door behind him and leaned against it. He hated the distressed look on her face. He wanted to help—if she'd let him. More and more frequently lately, he could feel her pushing him away, trying not to get too involved with him. He was doing the same, but it was getting harder and harder to keep his distance—physically, emotionally. Especially when she looked so badly in need of a hug, a soft word of comfort. Keeping his voice casual, he said, "What's up?"

Hilary swallowed. "That was my lawyer." Her face was flushed as she got up to roam the small eight-by-ten-square-foot space restlessly. "Dash has been digging into Mrs. Jones's past. He found out she had a miscarriage when she was seventeen. Apparently she got pregnant out of wedlock, went to a home for unwed mothers and had a miscarriage there. She recovered and went back to high school, graduated with her class without most knowing what had happened to her. Rick, she never told me about that miscarriage." The betrayal she felt showed in her face.

He shared her anger, her disbelief. "If you'd known—"

"Right. It might have made all the difference in the outcome of her case. Certainly, I would have watched her more closely."

"Did her previous doctor suspect she had an incompetent cervix?"

"I don't know yet. Thus far, Dash has not been able to gain access to the medical records at the home. All he's been able to do is confirm unofficially that she was there and had a miscarriage early in the fourth month, same as the recent time."

"So what next?"

"He's going to try and get a court order that would allow us to subpoena the records. Barring that, he'll confront Mrs. Jones and her attorney privately, then try and get them to drop the malpractice suit." Rick was glad her trauma was almost over. He wanted her to believe in herself again. Yet he didn't want to lose her. So many times he had almost told her how he felt about her, that he was falling in love—hopelessly, irrevocably. So many times he'd fought the urge to drag her into his arms and kiss her senseless, but he hadn't because he didn't want to put that kind of pressure on her.

He knew he could get her into bed if he waited long enough. He also knew as things stood he didn't have a prayer of holding her, getting her to marry him. All because of where he lived. And that hurt. But it was also understandable. Appalachia was a hard place to try and scratch out a living. Hilary had always planned on having much, much more. The lawsuit against her had put her plans on hold, but he couldn't expect her to stay there forever. Not and be happy. And more than anything, he wanted Hilary to be happy.

"I hope it works out," he said finally, his voice sounding scratchy.

Hilary looked at him, her feelings veiled. "So do I."

Silence. Because she looked like she needed some encouragement, he said softly, "This time next week, you could be free and clear."

Hilary shrugged and went over to open the blinds. "Maybe."

"You think you won't be?"

She looked troubled. "I want to believe that." She shook her head, distressed. "Part of me even does. But then there's another side that's more skeptical. I keep wondering if maybe there was something there with Mrs. Jones, something I missed. And why was she afraid to tell me about the earlier miscarriage? I know she couldn't have forgotten it. Am I that inaccessible? What did I forget to say or do? Why didn't she tell me any of this when I took her medical history during her first office visit?"

"Hilary, you're very thorough—"

"I try to be, God knows, but there still must be something missing, something vital in my abilities as a physician."

"How can you say that?" He stared at her, dumbfounded.

"Easy. Look at what happened with Clara. She told me she didn't think she needed to be taking her insulin anymore. I should've realized she might try and skip a dose, watched for that or had someone help me. Instead, all I did was talk to her, tell her firmly not to even think about skipping a dose of insulin." Remembering, she shook her head in self-inflicted disgust.

It made him angry to see Hilary beating herself up like this. "That's all you could have done."

She pressed her lips together tightly, obliterating their softness. "It'd be easier if I could believe that."

Through listening to the exercise in doubt and self-pity, he crossed to her and took her by the shoulders. "Listen to me, Boston. You're not your patients' keeper. You're their physician, that's all. You can tell them what they should be doing, you can give them proper treatment, but that is the extent of your duty. Your patients have a right to make their own mistakes and decisions, and a responsibility to keep themselves well. You can't be everywhere and do everything. No one can."

Her frustration evident, she looked up at him, her eyes brimming with tears. "Oh, Rick, I want to be the best doctor around," she whispered. "But lately, I've lost faith. There are times like now when I feel like such a failure. A horrible, stupid failure."

"Don't say that," he said gruffly. Not caring they were in the office, he wrapped his arms around her and held her close. "You're not a failure. The doubts you're having are normal. Every physician has them once in a while."

She looked unconvinced. "I still feel like such a washout. I'm not sure I'll ever be able to get my confidence back."

"I'll help you." He wouldn't stop until he succeeded. Knowing there was only one way to convince her of that, he bent and touched his lips to hers, and once he'd tasted the sweetness of her mouth, he couldn't get enough of her. Even as she submitted to his need, she demanded. Wild, passionate thoughts exploded in his head. He had visions of dragging her down to the floor, undressing her slowly.... Her mouth seemed fused to his. He began to feel and see the layers of mystery, the depth of the woman inside, to have a sense of how she could give and give. And he knew then how much he needed her, the loving spirit that belonged to Hilary and Hilary alone.

Only a knock on the door and Becca's voice stopped them from letting the passion take them wherever it would. "Hey, doc. Shake a leg!" Becca called. "We've got a waiting room full of patients to see."

Reluctantly the kiss drew to a halt. Her taste still on his lips, Rick let Hilary go. Her eyes still had that soft, dreamy expression, the sense of wonder he felt. He knew she was shaken by what had just transpired between them. So was he. When had his feelings for her gotten that deep, that encompassing?

Shocked and silent, she continued to stare at him, to tremble.

"We'll continue this later," he said. And that was a promise he meant to keep.

HOURS LATER, Hilary still couldn't believe she had let it happen, that she had not only allowed Rick to kiss her that way but that she had kissed him back. Exciting as the revelation of the passion was, it was also frightening. She cared about him, might even be falling in love with him, but she didn't want to be hurt, and she knew she couldn't bear to hurt him. Yet that was all she could see happening if she let him make love to her.

What was she going to do?

If he touched her again, she sensed she would be as lost as she was earlier that day.

But what, then?

She didn't know, was almost afraid to think about it.

As if mirroring her gloomy, despondent mood, the rain continued unabated the rest of the day. She couldn't get over the way it came down. Or imagine what the torrent of moisture must be doing to the gravel and dirt roads that peppered much of the rural countryside. She found out, near closing time when they got a call from the county sheriff's office.

"Bad news, folks," Becca reported, as soon as she'd hung up the phone. "The creek is over its banks. All the bridges leading into and out of town are flooded. So, none of us except Rick can get home tonight."

Hilary looked at Rick, beginning to feel trapped and panicky. "She's kidding, isn't she?"

Rick frowned. "I wish I could say she was."

"Me, too." Becca added. "Unfortunately, this is just something else you'll have to get used to around here."

Hilary wasn't sure she could. "What about your children?" Hilary asked. At least, unlike Becca, she had no family to worry about.

Becca smiled, relieved. "Luckily Will was able to get home to them before the bridge near our home was washed out, so I don't have to worry about that."

Without warning, the door to the clinic opened. A gust of cool, damp air blew in. The three moved forward to see Emma Schwartz stagger in, another woman from the mine by her side. "Thank heaven you're here," the other woman gasped. "Emma's in labor."

"Uh-oh," Becca whispered behind Hilary, so only she could hear. "She's barely into her seventh month."

And they weren't equipped to handle the birth of a premature baby, Hilary knew. She moved forward, ready to lend a hand.

Emma recoiled immediately. Between pains, she snarled, "Don't touch me..." She sent Rick a beseeching look. "I swear to God, you let her lay a hand on me and I'll sue you and this clinic for all its worth. I heard about how you misdiagnosed Mary Lou Pritchart's little boy. Why, Stevie could've died because of you!"

Ignoring Emma's angry tirade, Becca eased her into the closest chair. "Now, now, calm down, honey. We'll get you taken care of. The most important thing for you to do right now is relax."

And she won't be able to do that with me in the room, Hilary thought, stung by the pregnant woman's criticism. A criticism she knew wasn't entirely without merit. Feeling the need to escape, she whirled and went back into her private office, her cheeks red with humiliation.

She was still there when Rick tracked her down five minutes later. "Sorry about that," he said, slipping into the room and shutting the door behind him. "She didn't know what she was saying."

Hilary lifted her chin. "I think she knew exactly what she was saying."

Rick paused, then evidently deciding not to sugarcoat the unpleasant situation, said, "Maybe so. At any rate, all the bridges between here and the Interstate are flooded out. We're going to have to deliver the baby here."

She stared at him disbelievingly. "Rick, that's crazy. That baby is going to need an incubator. And because of her eclampsia, Emma's own life is in danger."

He nodded gravely. "Precisely why I need your help."

Hilary was silent. She wanted to help. But she also knew it was an impossible situation. Emma didn't consider her capable. And in a high-risk situation such as this, it was vital Emma trust whoever delivered her baby.

Besides that, privately she still had her own doubts. She wondered if she would be able to pick up on the first minute signs of trouble. Was she as competent as she had once felt? What would happen if something went wrong? Could she live with the loss of another child? Suddenly, she didn't think so. What he was suggesting was just too risky. "Can't you call in a helicopter?" she asked agitatedly.

"The closest life-flight service is headquartered in Lexington. Becca's already alerted them, but Lexington is having fierce electrical storms, heavy wind shear and they can't help us out yet. They figure it'll be at least three or four hours before they can take off, and another half an hour to get here, depending on the weather."

The arrangement wasn't ideal, but it was better than nothing. If they could just get Emma to hold on until they could get her to a hospital, she and her baby would have an excellent chance of making it, Hilary knew. "Can you delay the birth?"

"Unfortunately, no. Emma wasn't kidding when she said she was in labor. She's already dilated eight centimeters. At the rate her labor is progressing, she'll deliver in the next half hour or so. Hilary, I need your help." He stressed the last sentence emotionally.

Hilary wanted to help, more than she'd wanted to do anything in her life. Recalling the way Emma had looked at her, she feared it wouldn't work. She made a small sound indicative of her inner turmoil. "What's her blood pressure now?"

To her dismay, Rick affirmed what she suspected, that it was already dangerously high. "Rick, if I go in there, I'll upset her. That'll make her blood pressure shoot up even more. Like it or not, you're going to have to go this alone. It's the only way. You know I'm right."

He faced her tensely. She could tell he was disappointed in her, but he also knew, because of Emma's attitude, she had no choice. "All right," he said finally, "I'll try, but if it's any more complicated I'm coming after you." He went quickly back to tend to Emma.

For the next fifteen minutes, Hilary paced back and forth in the reception area. She'd never felt more frustrated or helpless in her life, and it didn't help matters any that she could hear Emma moaning with pain in the next room.

Becca came out. Though normally a very competent, capable nurse, she looked frightened. "Hilary, Rick needs you. We're losing the baby. The heart rate has dropped to eighty and is fading fast. He thinks the cord is twisted around the baby's neck."

This time Hilary didn't have to think. She just moved. When she entered the examining room-cum-birthing center, Emma had her eyes closed and, in the midst of another strong contraction, was panting rapidly. As the top of the baby's head appeared, Hilary knew immediately what was wrong. The baby was in distress due to deprivation of oxygen, probably because the cord was wrapped around its neck.

Quickly she washed her hands and donned sterile gloves, then reached for the forceps.

Emma opened her eyes and started to protest. Knowing they had no time to argue if they were to save her baby's life, Hilary cut her off brusquely. "Your baby's in jeopardy, Emma. So do what I tell you."

The gravity of the situation must have penetrated Emma's pain-fogged mind, for she lapsed into tense silence. While Emma panted through another hard contraction, Hilary crowded her fingers alongside the head and gently felt for the two soft spots and the baby's ear. After accurately diagnosing the exact position of the baby's head, she gently and carefully applied the forceps. Sweat pouring down her face and into her eyes, she rotated the baby's head until it was in the proper position, then this accomplished, she began the extraction, pulling steadily for fifteen or twenty seconds, then releasing traction momentarily before she pulled again.

Little by little the baby's head emerged. Seeing where the baby's cord was wrapped around its neck, Hilary struggled to loosen it enough to pull the baby out.

The bluish color of the infant's skin alarmed her. Fortunately Rick was right there to help. No sooner was the baby out, than he was suctioning the infant's lungs.

With her airway cleared, the baby let out a howl of outrage.

Hilary clamped the cord three inches from the abdomen and cut. Joy and relief mingled to give her an unbeatable feeling of euphoria, one she was all too happy to be able to share. "You've got a girl, Emma," Hilary said emotionally, placing the baby on her stomach, so she could see. "A beautiful, healthy four-pound baby girl."

THE NEXT FEW HOURS were not easy ones. Because of her early birth, the little girl's ability to breathe on her own was impaired significantly. Working together Rick and Hilary constructed a makeshift incubator and monitored the flow of oxygen the child was receiving. Becca maintained a close eye on Emma, whose blood pressure had gone down almost immediately after the birth. When seven o'clock came and the helicopter arrived, all three staff members were exhausted.

"They'll both be fine," Rick said, as he and Hilary stood in the drizzling rain and watched the life-flight helicopter take off once again. Becca slipped back inside the clinic. Rick and Hilary were slower to leave the cool, fragrant rain.

"Thanks to you," Hilary said.

"And you." Rick wrapped an arm about her waist and drew her in close to his side. "I couldn't have done it without you."

"Sure you could have," she said lightly, knowing it was true. Rick was an excellent doctor. "It just wouldn't have been quite as easy."

He held open the door for her. "How did it feel to deliver a baby again?"

Hilary took a moment to savor the feeling as she stepped inside. She turned to face Rick, surprised to realize now it was all over, she hadn't once suffered any doubts. There'd been no time and no reason. "It felt good," she said happily. "Although the lack of facilities and emergency equipment is a constant aggravation. If that baby'd had heart trouble, Rick, we would've lost her for sure." And that was something Hilary knew she just couldn't deal with.

He nodded gravely, raindrops still glistening on his wheat-blond hair. "I know. Fortunately we don't get flooded out and have to deliver a baby here except once in a great while."

To lose even one baby because of lack of facilities would be too much for Hilary. She frowned, wishing more could be done.

Becca came out into the waiting room, her overcoat on, her umbrella and purse in hand. "Well, I don't know about you two, but I'm going to walk down the street to my girlfriend's house and spend the night there. It's got to be more comfortable than the clinic sofa."

They laughed and said goodnight. She left.

Rick ran a hand over his jaw and looked at the hard linoleum floor, the single vinyl waiting-room sofa. Hilary knew what he was thinking, it didn't look very comfortable.

"Your house is impossible to get to with the bridges out," he said easily. "But we can still make it to mine. Want to go?"

He had kissed her passionately just that morning, but there was nothing sexual in his eyes now. Only tenderness, friendship, the wish to celebrate a truly remarkable birth and her unexpected reentry, however legally foolhardy, into obstetrics.

Knowing this moment wouldn't come again, she smiled. After the day she'd had, a night on his sofa would be heaven. "Sure," she said easily. "Just let me get my coat."

Chapter Eleven

"You look happy," Rick observed, as the two of them shed their rain gear and muddy boots just inside his foyer.

"I am." Hilary grinned back at him. Although the drive to his place had been a rough one, filled with close calls on the muddy, rain-drenched roads, they had finally made it—without once getting stuck in the mud. Outside, the rain was still coming down hard and fast. It made being inside the cool, dark house all the more cozy. She watched as Rick walked around turning on one light after another. Shivering with the drop in temperature, she followed him, her socks moving silently on the polished wood floors.

"I'd forgotten how much I like delivering babies."

Rick knelt before the fireplace. Although it was still August, it was definitely a night for a fire in the grate, and she watched appreciatively as he rolled newspaper and placed three logs in the grate. He worked quickly, expertly. The fire was going in less than three minutes. "You were great with Emma, by the way," he said, his attention turning back to her as he replaced the screen. "For a moment I didn't know if she was going to let you help."

Still cold, Hilary bypassed the thick red-and-white sofas in favor of the open space next to the hearth. She sank down on the floor, sitting cross-legged before him. Only when the fire was warming her chilled body, did she continue their conversation about Emma. "It was no secret she would rather have had someone else." Hilary sighed remembering how much Emma's threats to sue her had hurt, and brought her knees up to her chest. "At any rate, all's well that ends well. Both mother and baby should do just fine."

Rick walked over to the bar and poured them each a small glass of wine. He carried the glasses back to where she was sitting, and after handing her hers, stretched out on the floor beside her. "I know I didn't say it earlier, but thanks for helping me out." Their glasses clinked as he touched his glass to hers in silent toast. They sipped their wine simultaneously, their eyes holding, caressing. His voice was even softer when he spoke again. "I know it wasn't easy for you to put your own career on the line to do that."

Hilary took another swallow of wine, aware the shivers coursing down her spine now had nothing to do with the rising temperature in the room. "I admit it made me nervous to take care of her when she was so opposed to my doing so." She fell silent, staring at the licking orange and yellow flames of the fire. Her voice was softer, lower, when she turned back to Rick. As the wine hit her empty stomach, she felt her skin take on a warm glow that was in direct contrast to her unnerved state earlier. She had never been so scared as she was when she walked into that makeshift delivery room, knowing the outcome—indeed the life of Emma's baby—depended on her skill and her skill alone.

Rick was still watching her curiously, trying to understand. Hilary sighed and feeling closer to him than ever, explained why that evening's delivery had been particularly hard for her. "In the past my services as a physician were always appreciated. I was always trusted. It didn't help matters any knowing Emma had threatened to sue me if anything went wrong and that I had no insurance to cover me if anything did go wrong." As it might very well have. "Had that happened, there's no way I could pay off a million-dollar settlement, and it's unlikely a judge or jury would be sympathetic to the idea of me practicing without insurance—when I'd been put on probation at Boston General for a similar situation."

Hilary finished her wine and set her glass aside before adding to her wish list. "Of course, it would've been a lot easier to take that risk had we been in a fully equipped neonatal and obstetrical-care unit."

Rick got to his feet and held out his hand. Hilary took it, continuing as he drew her gently to her feet and the sofa. "We would've been in trouble if we'd ended up doing a C-section."

"I know," he commiserated gently.

They stayed up a little while longer, talking about everything and anything. Finally, exhausted, emotionally worn out but not at all sleepy, she stifled a yawn. She knew if she didn't get some sleep she would feel it in spades tomorrow. "I think I had better go to bed," she said casually. "You said I could bunk on your sofa?"

"Or my bed, if you prefer." He got up to poke at the fire.

For once, Hilary was glad she couldn't see his face. Sleep in his sheets, in his bed? No thanks. It was going to be hard enough getting to sleep in his house, knowing he was just a few hundred feet away from her. "I don't want to put you out," she said as politely as she could manage. "The sofa will be fine."

He nodded, content to give her space.

Hours later, however, Hilary was still awake. Lying on the sofa, she watched the glowing embers of the fire. She wondered if Rick was asleep or awake upstairs. She wondered if he was as lonely right now as she was. She wondered if he still wanted her even half as much as she wanted him.

She wondered if they would ever get together, and how she would feel if they did, and then she had to leave him.

THE RAINS STOPPED during the night. The clinic was full the next morning of people with injuries or illnesses directly or indirectly related to the storm. Hilary and Rick worked at a mad pace all through lunch and straight up until closing. When five o'clock came they collapsed in near exhaustion.

"The road to your place is still out," Rick pointed out.

"You could come to my place and spend the night," Becca said. "Will called a little while ago. He said the creek is down enough to make the bridge passable."

"Wouldn't she be putting one of your kids out of a bed, though?" Rick asked guilelessly.

Hilary looked at Rick, surprised he would be so obvious in his attempt to have a say in her plans. Becca sent him an amused look before she arched a brow and responded drily, "Yes, but they've roughed it before." She paused, looking from Rick to Hilary and back to Rick again. "I suppose your place has so much more room, though, doesn't it, Rick?" she said drily.

Why do I have the feeling I'm about to be seduced? Hilary thought. She'd been with Rick last night; he hadn't tried anything past one soul-satisfying kiss in his kitchen. When it had threatened to get out of hand, they'd called a halt by mutual consent and both of them had taken it in stride, realizing they both still needed time to think. He hadn't so much as laid a finger on her since, not all morning or all afternoon. Yet the way he was looking at her suddenly made her think he was fantasizing about kissing her again. And again.

"That's true," Rick continued easily, suddenly very interested in sorting through the stack of mail in his hand. "My place does have plenty of room." He looked up at her. "Hilary? It's up to you."

I'd be safer with Becca and Will but have more fun with Rick. That quickly, her decision was made. "I'll stay at Rick's, I guess. It'll probably make things simpler for you, Becca. Besides, Will and the kids probably want to spend time with you since they haven't seen you for over thirty-six hours."

"You're probably right about that." Becca slipped out of her lab coat and unlaced the stethoscope from around her neck. "All four of them will probably be vying for my attention all night."

Rick's eyes sparkled. "Have fun," he said.

"And you two behave yourselves!" Becca said, as she slipped out the front door.

Rick turned to Hilary, feigning bewilderment. "What'd she mean by that?"

Hilary shrugged, shucking her own lab coat. She felt suddenly shy and nervous, compelled to cover it with a joke. "Beats me. I'm a perfect house guest."

He grinned and stretched lazily before tossing down the mail, his steady gaze holding her enthralled. "I know." He stepped toward her and her heartbeat accelerated. "What do you say we go home?"

Home. She hadn't known one word could sound so sweet.

What would it be like to live with Rick? Hilary wondered. He was certainly domestic enough, an accomplished carpenter, general fix-it man and cook. He kept a clean, well-ordered house. He was easygoing, cheerful in the morning. What was there not to like?

Maybe that was what bothered her. The idea of living with him, even temporarily, was all too enticing.

NO SOONER HAD THEY gotten to Rick's, when his doorbell rang. Hilary went to answer it. What confronted her stunned her. In the weeks since his brother's elopement, Hilary hadn't heard a word of Kenny and Daisy. Now the couple who'd caused such turmoil weeks ago stood before her, looking sheepish and embarrassed. "Kenny. Daisy," she cried. Impulsively, she hugged them both. "Welcome home."

Kenny smiled shyly. "Thanks. It's good to see you, too, doc. Is my brother around?"

"He's in the kitchen."

Rick was as surprised as Hilary had been to see his brother. Unfortunately his reaction wasn't one of exclusive delight. The two men faced one another awkwardly.

In the end, Kenny was the first to speak. "Daisy and I heard about the storms here. We had to get back to see if everyone was all right. We can't get to Mom's yet, though. The bridge between her house and town is still out.''

"I know,'' Rick said.

"If the bridge between here and Will's wasn't open, we wouldn't have been able to get here.''

"Have you talked to Mom?'' Rick asked, his expression still slightly tense.

Kenny nodded. "I called her from the general store. She thought maybe we could stay with you, for just a day or two anyway, until the creek goes down.''

Rick glanced at the wedding rings on both their hands, then said in a scrupulously polite tone, "That'd be fine.''

Kenny gave a sigh of relief. Daisy was less certain. "We don't want to impose—''

Rick sighed. "Look, it's no secret I didn't want the two of you to get married before you started college.''

"Plenty of other people around here do it,'' Kenny piped up.

"That's true—but lots of them never finish college or even get there as a result. Dad wanted you to have an education.''

"He also wanted me to be happy,'' Kenny retorted fiercely. He reached over to take Daisy's hand. "And we are happy, Rick.''

Hilary could see that they were. She sensed Rick intuited that too, though, judging from the implacable look on his features, he wasn't quite ready to admit that to himself.

"I'm going to college, Rick, just as soon as Daisy finishes up," Kenny promised.

Hilary wanted to say something, but kept quiet when she sensed Rick's tension.

"Actually," Daisy interjected with shy pride, almost naive, "Kenny is going to try and get into the ROTC program. He's already been tested by the Army. They're just waiting on the paperwork to make it official. If it goes through in time, he'll start with me. If not, he'll have to wait until next fall, but one way or another he is going to get his education."

Hilary was too stunned to speak.

Daisy continued fiercely, "Furthermore, we are responsible enough to be married, Rick. And we proved it this past month in Myrtle Beach. We both worked double shifts at a beach resort and saved practically everything we made, including tips. We've got a thousand dollars in the bank between us now. To help with our college expenses. Furthermore, I've applied for student loans to pay my tuition. I don't want Kenny supporting me any more than you do."

"Daisy, that's enough," Kenny said, aggravated and embarrassed. "You don't have to defend us to him."

"But I want to!" Daisy cried. "I don't want him hating me or thinking I've ruined your life."

If anything, Hilary thought, Daisy had gotten Kenny back on track.

"I don't hate you, Daisy," Rick said, chastened. "And I never did. I can't say I'm thrilled with my brother going into the army—but, well, I've had time to think it over, and I realize you're old enough to make your own decisions. I was just worried." He held out his hand. "Truce?"

Daisy's lower lip quavered and her eyes filled with tears. "Really?"

"Really," Rick said gently. Moving forward, Rick took her into his arms for a conciliatory hug. "I'm sorry," he said to his brother, hugging him, too. Tears misted everyone's eyes.

"You were great with Kenny and Daisy today," Hilary said later that evening, after they'd finished dinner and Kenny and Daisy had retired to his loft.

Rick had decided to bunk down in the living room with Hilary. The temperature had already warmed, making a fire out of the question. The atmosphere of the living room was no less intimate, though. She felt relaxed, cossetted. As if the two of them were on a camping expedition that had limitless possibilities. She knew in another day the bridge would be clear of flood water again and she would probably be able to get back to her house. The thought depressed her unutterably. As fanciful as this time with him was, she didn't want it to end.

He smiled at her. "It was nice to see they were doing okay."

She looked over at him, feeling unexpectedly sentimental. His face was shadowed by a day's growth of beard. He looked relaxed and at ease in the T-shirt and pajama bottoms he had chosen to wear to bed.

With effort, she turned her thoughts back to the conversation they'd been having about Kenny and Daisy. "They do love each other, Rick," she said softly.

"Yeah, I know. It's funny." He closed his eyes. "At eighteen, he has everything I want. A wife who loves him—"

Someone who would be happy living here in Appalachia and not feel trapped, Hilary thought.

"—the prospect for a rich, full family life."

Hilary smiled sadly. "I guess some get contentment early." A trace of homesickness crept into her voice.

Hearing it, Rick took a long, pained look at her and said, "You miss Boston, don't you?"

Hilary nodded and turned onto her side, facing him. Although Rick was only five or six feet away, stretched out in a sleeping bag on the floor, she felt as if he were a million miles away. "I've never been away from the East for so long. It seems strange."

"Maybe Dash will call soon with news about your case."

"Maybe." But that didn't make her as happy as she felt she ought to be, either. Because she knew when that happened she would have to go back home, to the life she had painstakingly carved out for herself. Otherwise, she'd always have doubts. She'd always wonder if she could have succeeded there if only she'd tried a second time. Knowing that, she couldn't get involved with him, or start something that in the end would only end up hurting them both. They were friends now, increasingly good friends. They would have to be satisfied with that.

"It's just like Mom to insist they go through with the wedding anyway," Rick said several days later, from the pastor's study in the small country chapel.

Hilary straightened his bow tie, knowing in a few minutes she had to join the other guests. The past few days had been crazy with work. "I'm really glad you agreed to be Kenny's best man."

"I couldn't let him down."

She smiled sympathetically. There was no doubt in her mind how devoted Rick was to his family. "I know."

Rick looked resplendent in his tux, and as she studied him she felt a rush of desire mingling with an unprecedented feeling of contentment.

Rick wrapped an arm about her shoulders and pulled her near. "Well, you ready?"

"I hope so," she murmured.

Behind them, the door banged open. "Dr. Hilary! Dr. Rick! How do I look?" Clementine asked, as she raced in to join them.

Hilary grinned at the bundle of energy. "Just gorgeous!" she decided promptly, stopping to adjust the pale blue satin bow that had gotten off-center in Clementine's hair.

"I'm going to be the best flower girl there ever was!" Clementine vowed excitedly.

"I know you will," Hilary said, and then on impulse bent down to give the precocious child a hug. "Just remember to walk slowly when you're coming up the aisle."

"I know, I know." On tiptoe, Clementine pranced forward with a deliberate, princess-like gait. Gone was the uncared-for waif Hilary had met earlier in the summer; in her place was a little girl who received boundless attention from every source.

I'll miss her, if I leave, Hilary thought sadly. And Mrs. Orlansky, too—whom Hilary visited twice weekly in the Lexington hospital where she was still recuperating from her fall.

In the back of the small community church, the organ sounded. Hilary wished both her comrades good luck, and then went forward to take a seat. At Alva's insistence, she sat in the front pew reserved for Kenny's family. Alva clutched a lace handkerchief. "I always cry at weddings," she whispered to Hilary, her eyes already blurring with tears. "So don't mind me."

Hilary reached over and squeezed Alva's hand. She had never been one to cry at weddings before, but tonight she was feeling strangely sentimental. And very sad, suddenly. Like maybe she had missed out on an awful lot of life by not being married.

In the front of the church, next to the choir, the organist began to play. Rick and Kenny entered from the side door and stood beside the minister, both looking tall and proud and impossibly handsome.

The ceremony was beautiful and old-fashioned, but all Hilary was conscious of as Daisy and Kenny promised to love, honor and cherish one another, was Rick, standing beside Kenny. He kept glancing back at her, too, as if unable to help himself.

Finally it was over. The happy couple was marching triumphantly back down the aisle. Rick grabbed her hand as he passed her and drew her into the receiving line at the front of the church. "You've been such a champion of the two lovebirds all along, you deserve to be here, too."

"Face it, big brother," Kenny teased. "You just want her standing beside you."

Rick laughed, and didn't deny it.

Later, at the reception at Alva's home, gaiety abounded. A group of fiddlers played lively tunes and haunting ballads.

Guests flowed out of the house and onto the lawn, many Hilary had met, many she had not. Everyone there had brought a dish or two, and the spread was incredible.

She hated to leave when the party wound down at midnight and Rick drove her home. For the first time in her life she wondered if she had sacrificed too much in becoming a doctor. She feared the demands of her job, the long hours, the hardships, would keep her from ever having a satisfying personal life of her own. As much as she loved being a doctor, she wanted more out of life. *Was that so wrong? Was it selfish?*

She had no answer.

Rick too was unusually subdued as he parked his truck in her drive. *He realizes my time here is about over, too,* she thought, a wave of unbearable sadness coming over her. Feeling inexplicably near tears, she was about to get out of the truck when he stopped her, a gentle hand to her arm. "You can't forget this."

"Forget what?"

He reached behind his seat, and expending very little energy, brought out a small plastic container. "This. It's a piece of wedding cake to put under your pillow."

"You're kidding."

"Nope, it's an old custom around here. Single women take a piece of cake and put it under their pillow. They sleep on it at night and then their wishes are supposed to come true."

Hilary rolled her eyes. If he was relegating her to the category of old maid, even in teasing, he was in trouble. "Don't tell me you believe that."

She got slowly out of the truck. He joined her in the walk up to her front porch. "That's not important. The question is do you?"

She unlocked the door and flipped on the light. She shook her head in bemusement. "I don't know. All I can visualize getting out of it is one very squashed piece of cake, and maybe, just maybe, a little icing in my hair.'' Considering the restless way she had been sleeping lately, that was a very definite possibility.

"Trust me. You don't have to worry about that. That's already been taken care of." Unsnapping the lid on the single serving container, he showed her the piece of white cake with the pink roses had already been wrapped in plastic wrap. Gently he lifted the piece of cake out of the container and set it aside. "I'm nothing if not prepared."

"I can see that," she said drily. "Who did that for you? Your mother?"

"Daisy. Now," he said, grinning as he started for her bedroom, "which side of the bed do you sleep on?"

He obviously knew she wouldn't bother doing this if left to her own devices. Amused, and seeing no way out of this ridiculously silly situation save to suffer through it, Hilary pointed to the left. "Right there."

"Allow me." He turned back the spread and lifted the pillow, sliding the piece of cake next to the bottom sheet. He put the pillow gingerly back into place. "All set."

"I can't believe we're doing this," she moaned.

Rick took her by the shoulders and closely examined the look on her face. "Don't believe in superstition, hmm?" he teased in a soft, mellow baritone.

"Not this one."

He took her hand as they walked back out of the bedroom, his fingers curling possessively around hers. "Well, I hope the tradition works, anyway," he murmured as he paused to say goodnight to her at the front door. "Because if anyone deserves to have her dreams come true, it's you."

Was this Rick's way of telling her they could never be together? The emotional side of her wished it weren't so...and noted the moment of pained expression in his eyes, before he leaned over and kissed her forehead.

Then he turned and went out the door.

Chapter Twelve

"Good news, kiddo, you're home free. They've dropped the lawsuit."

Hilary took a moment to comprehend what Dash was saying. She sat on the edge of her desk at the clinic, aware that Rick was next door.

Hilary sighed, relief and pain flooding over her. Her breath trembled out. "It's been so long since I'd heard from you, I thought we'd headed down a blind alley."

Dash's voice gentled. "Sorry about that, but I wanted to wait until I had some positive news for you before we talked again. It took a week to get a subpoena from the judge. Once I had the medical records of her diagnosis I arranged a meeting with Mrs. Jones after she returned from overseas. She's been there the last three months giving a seminar for MIT. We could've handled it via transatlantic conference calls, but I thought this was better done face-to-face."

Dash's voice was so brisk, so businesslike. Hilary felt herself beginning to relax. Men didn't get any sharper than Dash. "I agree," Hilary said.

If Dash's plan had worked, and it sounded like it had, then she would be free to leave soon.

"Anyway, I'm glad I waited until she got back," Dash continued, his voice taking on a harder edge. "It turned out her husband didn't know anything about her previous pregnancy or miscarriage. That's why she didn't tell you that part of her medical history. She didn't want him to know. But when I confronted her with the knowledge our investigators uncovered, there was no denying it was true. She broke down, sobbed." Dash paused. A hint of regret crept into his voice. "That was one bad scene, Hil."

Hilary could imagine it had been traumatic, but so had her experience being sued. Her mind already moving ahead, wanting to work out every detail of the puzzle, Hilary asked, "What about her absences, Dash? Were they just due to morning sickness, or was it something else?"

His voice dropped another soothing notch. "You were right there, too. She was having twinges, a little staining. Remembering what happened before, she was scared out of her mind. Scared you would be able to tell she'd been pregnant before and had lost the baby, if she went in to see you. So she stayed home, stayed in bed. After a few days, the twinges went away, so did the staining. She thought she'd be fine, and she was for several weeks until the day of the miscarriage.''

Hilary slowly expelled the breath she'd been holding. ''If she'd told me the truth from the outset, we could have saved her baby.'' That thought saddened her terribly.

''She knows that, too.''

Silence fell between them. Although she was still fuming over the unjustness of all she'd been put through, the unnecessariness of it all, she also knew there was no use railing over the past. It had happened. It was over. They all had to go forward and learn from this experience. She knew she had. She would never let a patient get away with missing or putting off appointments again.

''Anyway, on the brighter side, now that you're free and clear, your malpractice insurance coverage has been reinstated, at no increased price, by the way. The hospital wants you back—ASAP. A friend of mine is writing up the whole story. It'll appear in tomorrow's paper. The television stations here want to interview you right away and I think it's a good idea, Hilary. The sooner the word is out that you were erroneously accused, the sooner you can get back your thriving medical practice.''

The thought didn't excite her the way it would have three months ago. ''I see.''

Ignoring the hesitation in her voice, Dash went on cheerfully, "I've booked you on a flight this afternoon."

Hilary did a double take. "That's not much notice."

"You have to act now. We want people to know you're back one hundred percent. We want them to see that you're in great shape and that the hospital is wasting no time in standing behind you, now that the truth is finally out."

Hilary knew Dash was right. Her indictment had been big news among her colleagues. It was only fair her vindication be treated with the same newsworthiness. And she did so want to clear her name, unsully her reputation. She had hated leaving Boston in shame. As much as she hated to leave Rick right now, she knew she had no choice if she ever wanted to get her professional life back in order. "I'll be back," she said swallowing. "But I need a few days." She again glanced toward Rick's office. "I have clients here."

She heard him sigh and knew she'd won. "Okay, Hil. But don't linger too long. We all want you back, pronto."

"Pronto," she said, setting the phone down on its cradle. Somehow her heart did not feel a reprieve.

"SO YOU'RE GOING, just like that." His words were heavy with indictment.

"I have no choice." She'd gone into Rick's office immediately. She felt guilty as hell for leaving without so much as two weeks' notice.

He stared at her uncomprehendingly, then shook his head, making no effort to hide his bitterness. "Don't kid yourself. You have a choice, Hil. You just can't wait to get out of here, can you?"

"You're being unfair," she said thickly.

They'd known this was coming. No regrets, she reminded herself firmly. *They'd come to the end of the line. They'd known it was there when she started working here.*

He turned to her, a wealth of feeling in his silver eyes. "I know the initial arrangement was temporary, but you could stay on here, you know—" he countered, giving her a long steady look. But he stopped, and after a moment turned to her. He swallowed his hurt pride. "All right Hilary—whatever you decide. Do you need help packing?"

She stepped back, surprised how his sudden acquiescence hurt her. She nodded. "It'd help. In the meantime I can prepare my patients."

"Okay. We'll be over tomorrow to start. Right now we have to get back to the examination rooms."

With that he walked out of the room—and out of her life forever.

HILARY WAS STANDING at the nurses' station, updating orders on one of her patients when the chief of staff stopped by to talk to her. "I heard the Greenbaum twins are okay," Dr. Lynn Whitfield said.

"Yeah," Hilary grinned, snapping the lid shut on her chart. "I didn't know if they were both going to make it . . . but they're doing fine now."

"But you did it," Dr. Whitfield said, grinning.

"Yeah, I did." Hilary smiled back. She glanced over at some of the labor and delivery nurses working behind the desk. "Of course it helped to have the best staff in the city assisting." Not to mention a wealth of high-tech equipment at her disposal. No doubt about it, Boston General was a great place to work.

"Well, it's nice to have you back," Dr. Whitfield said.

"It's nice to be back," Hilary countered, though the truth was she felt sad. Yet since she had returned it seemed everything had worked in her favor. Her name had been cleared, her practice was picking up again. She had her confidence back. On a practical and professional level, she had everything she had ever wanted and more, the confidence that came with knowing she could tend patients with much, much less.

So why was it suddenly not enough? Why did the glamor of the city seem less vital to her well-being than before? Was it because she had grown since being away, or because her values, the focus of her existence had changed? Being the best physician she could possibly be was still important to her, but she was no

longer certain that meant being a big-city doctor.
Maybe it simply meant being needed, helping people,
knowing your presence made a difference...saved
lives...

She knew she was doing a good job here, but she
wasn't indispensable. There were any of a dozen
doctors who could step in to take her place at a moment's notice and her patients would be okay. That
wasn't the case in Kentucky.

She knew Rick felt that she had abandoned them,
leaving the way she had, without at least waiting
around for however long it took him to get a replace-
ment with obstetrical training. Of course he hadn't
been that blunt, but she'd seen it in his eyes. Away
long enough to get perspective, she felt he might be
right about that. Unfortunately her wisdom had come
too late.

Finished with her paperwork, Hilary handed the
chart back to the nursing supervisor and headed for
her private office on the eighth floor.

"You've got a long-distance phone call," her sec-
retary said as Hilary passed.

Hilary's brow furrowed. She wasn't expecting anyone. Going on into her office, she was surprised to
hear Rick's voice on the other end of the line. "I'm
calling about Clara Orlansky." It was Rick. Any joy
she felt abated. In a brisk, businesslike tone, Rick explained the trouble he'd been having with her, con-
cluding, "She's just not doing anything she's supposed

to. She's not walking as much as she should or following her prescribed diet, and now I suspect she isn't taking her medicine on schedule, either.''

''Why not?'' Hilary asked, alarmed. She had been so sure after Clara's fall, that she had learned her lesson about that. Maintaining her blood-sugar levels was extremely important, lest Clara lapse into a diabetic coma or become confused and wander off again.

''I'm not sure. She has all sorts of excuses, of course—she didn't feel like walking or she didn't think eating just one piece of extra-rich pecan pie would hurt or she just knew she didn't need her medicine until much later—''

''But that's not it, is it?'' Hilary said, depressed.

''No,'' Rick agreed. He emitted a lengthy breath. ''I hate to say this . . . to even think it, but I think she's given up.'' His hurt and frustration were evident in his low tone. ''I don't think she wants to live anymore.''

''Oh, no. Rick—''

''Anyway, that's why I called,'' he continued more brusquely than ever, cutting her short. ''You were always so good to her, and you're also about the only person she'll listen to, at all. I thought maybe if you telephone her, if you put in a good word for me, she might reconsider and let me take care of her. Because if she doesn't start doing what I tell her, then she isn't going to be around a whole lot longer.''

''Of course I'll talk to her for you,'' she said, knowing the situation had to be very bad for Rick to call her. Knowing what a cantankerous person Clara could be, however, she knew it wouldn't be easy to get her to cooperate. "More than once, if necessary," Hilary added.

An awkward silence fell between them, interrupted only by the static on the long-distance line. She was dismayed to find once his business had been concluded, Rick had nothing more to say to her of a personal nature. They'd been so close once, but her leaving him had destroyed all that. She swallowed hard, determined to keep the emotion out of her voice. "Is everything else okay?" she asked pragmatically.

"Yeah, fine," he said, in an unenthusiastic tone. "Listen, I gotta go. I appreciate your helping me out with Clara—"

"No problem."

"'Bye."

The receiver clicked. Hilary stared at it a moment before putting it down. Tears filled her eyes and overflowed down her cheeks. But for once she could do nothing to stop them.

Later, she called Clara. Clara was no more receptive to her overtures of friendship and concern than Rick had been. Hilary tried her best to convince Clara to let Rick take care of her, or at least take care of herself, but she knew her advice was falling on deaf ears.

Feeling more despondent than ever, Hilary dialed the clinic. She explained to Rick what had happened.

"I tried my best, but I'm afraid it didn't do any good."

He was silent, and when he spoke again unhappiness radiated in his voice. "Yeah, well...I guess I should've known."

Unable to stand the thought of anything happening to Clara, Hilary persisted. "Has Becca talked to her?"

"Yep. Will, too. So has everyone else I could think of, to no avail. She just...won't listen anymore." He sighed again heavily.

"Rick—"

"Listen, I appreciate your efforts, Hilary, and I know you did what you could, but I probably shouldn't have involved you in this in the first place. It isn't your problem anymore."

"Rick—"

He waited.

Tears filled her eyes again and it was all she could do to choke back a sob. With effort she composed herself and spoke again, "I really am sorry."

"I know. So am I." Again, they said goodbye.

Hilary was up most of the night, thinking about Clara, worrying, wondering, wishing there was more she could do. By the time she got to the hospital the next morning, she had shadows of strain under her eyes, and none of her usual buoyancy in her walk. Dr. Lynn Whitfield caught up with her in the hall. "I didn't think you were in last night," she said conversationally, giving Hilary a concerned look.

"I wasn't."

"Then what gives? Come on, Hil. Something's going on. I know you."

Knowing she had to talk to someone, Hilary briefly explained what had transpired the previous day, and how worried she still was about Clara. Dr. Whitfield listened sympathetically. After Hilary had concluded, she said, "Rick's right. Mrs. Orlansky isn't your problem anymore."

She shook her head in mute disagreement. "You don't understand. Clara doesn't have anyone."

"It sounds to me like she has Rick and Will and Becca."

"Yes, but... they don't understand her."

The chief of staff studied her calmly. "You've got to let go, Hilary. Your stint in Kentucky is behind you. Let the doctors there handle their own problems. You need to concentrate on your patients here."

Hilary knew Dr. Whitfield was right. From a professional standpoint there really was no reason for her to be worrying about patients no longer in her domain. But as the day passed and she couldn't get Clara off her mind, she knew, like it or not, that she owed Clara more than anyone in Boston could ever understand. Because of Clara, people had gained faith in her abilities as a physician. Because of Clara, Hilary had regained faith in herself.

She couldn't just let it end this way. She couldn't. Clara was too wonderful a person for that.

She also knew, where the cantankerous Clara was concerned, that a simple long-distance phone call—or even two or three—just wasn't going to cut it. She would have to go down and see her in person, look her straight in the face and convince her she needed to take the medical care offered her. Hilary could afford the trip. Something urged her on.

After arranging for another doctor to cover for her, Hilary booked a seat on the first flight out the following morning. By noon she was in Kentucky; an hour and a half later, she was in Crossings.

She couldn't face Rick just yet, so she drove the familiar country roads out to Clara's place, bordered on either side by trees awash in brilliant autumn colors of gold, red and orange. She felt a wave of homesickness engulf her. It was all she could do to blink back the tears.

She hadn't realized how much she had missed Kentucky until now.

Clara was on her front porch, her cane across her lap, when Hilary drove up. Her look of joy and surprise faded, though, as Hilary got out of the rental car, and medical bag in hand, started up the walk. "Don't expect me to get out the tea for you, missy," Clara said.

Her eyes stinging, Hilary continued up the walk. Her glance was both challenging and coaxing. "Why not, Clara?"

"Because I'm mad at you, that's why!" Clara remained in her rocking chair, but waved her cane at Hilary.

Hilary sat down on the railing, put her hands on either side of her, knowing this was the easy part. It was talking sense into her patient that was going to be the difficult part. "How come?"

"You left us."

It was on the tip of Hilary's tongue to explain again all the reasons why she'd had to leave. She stopped and bowed her head. When she looked at Clara again, she made no effort to hide her regret about that. "I know. I'm sorry." *I was such a fool.*

"None of them doctors in these parts are as good as you!"

"Now, I don't know about that—"

"It's true," Clara retorted. "They don't have your understanding of women problems."

Clara's medical problems didn't have anything at all to do with being female, but Hilary knew better than to point that out. After a moment, she asked cautiously, "Would it help if I could find a female doctor from another neighboring county to come out and take care of you?"

Clara looked at Hilary suspiciously. "Why would you want to do that?"

Hilary smiled, not the least bit put-off by the elderly woman's churlish attitude. She could see she was as near tears as Hilary felt. "Because I care about you,

Clara." This time, there was no disguising the lump of emotion in her throat.

Clara dashed at her eyes with the back of her hands. "Is that so? Then how come you left me, left all of us here?" She waved her cane again, punctuating the air with her statements. "We all thought you was happy here!"

"I was!"

"Becoming one of us!"

"I was!"

"Like family!"

That was true, too. Too choked up to speak, Hilary remained silent.

"Then why did you up and leave?" Clara asked.

Suddenly Hilary didn't know. It seemed she had thrown away everything in life that counted, to go back to a high-powered career that no longer mattered, not the way it had. "I don't know," she said finally, and the tears spilled down her cheeks.

Clara started to cry, too. After a while, she said gruffly, "If it'll get you to stop nagging me, I'll see another doctor...but only a lady one, y'hear? No more men coming out here to boss me around."

"I'll talk to Rick," Hilary promised.

After that, the afternoon passed blissfully enough. Clara let Hilary examine her, listened to a repeated lecture on the importance of sticking to her diet and taking her medication at the regularly prescribed intervals. Hilary walked with her, and again reminded

Clara how important it was to walk and keep walking at her age, to prevent her muscles from atrophying and becoming useless. "You need the physical exercise."

"So do you," Clara bantered back sassily, sounding like her old self. "You're looking a little peaked."

"Thanks for the diagnosis," Hilary said, laughing.

With reluctance, Hilary finally left around supper time. She drove back into town. Rick's truck was in front of the clinic, but there were no other cars in sight. Knowing it was now or never, Hilary parked and went in.

At the sound of the door opening, he came halfway out into the hall. He stared at her, stunned. She stared back, feeling numb and scared. Finally she got it together enough to speak. "I came to see Clara. She wants a woman doctor. If she gets one, she promises to cooperate."

Rick blinked. "Great. I'll . . . uh, get right on it."

"Well..." she shrugged, feeling completely at a loss. There was so much to say. And so little. Her heart was telling her to run to him, her brain was telling her it was much too late.

He took two steps nearer, unlacing the stethoscope around his neck as he moved. "Going back?"

She took a deep steadying breath, then managed to answer with a modicum of calm, "Yes. In the morning."

"And in the meantime?"

"I'm staying at a hotel in Lexington."

"I see." He paused, his eyes roving her face dispassionately before settling again on her eyes with mesmerizing intensity. "You could have stayed here, you know. With one of us. My mom or whoever. Saved yourself a hotel bill."

Not with him, she couldn't have. Just one more time in his arms…one more embrace…and she knew she would never ever be able to leave again. Not even if he wanted her to go. Feeling the awkwardness draw out untenably, she said, "Thanks, but—"

"I understand," he interjected gruffly. "It's probably a lot nicer, more luxurious in a hotel."

Her spine stiffened. *That wasn't it, at all.* "I didn't want to impose." Her words were clearly enunciated.

He nodded. "Sure." He didn't sound convinced.

She turned, sure this had been a mistake. "I've got to go."

She was almost to the door when his voice stopped her. "Hil—" She turned, her hand on the knob. He swallowed awkwardly and ran a hand through his thick wheat-blond hair. "I—how's your job?"

She heaved a small sigh of relief. She hadn't wanted to leave things tense, either. They'd been so close once—and lost everything when she left. *Couldn't they at least be friends again?* "It's okay."

"Just okay?"

She shrugged. "It's a lot different from working here."

He continued to watch her carefully. "Better or worse?"

"Both." Another silence, this one even more strained than the last. "Did you find another doctor for the clinic yet?" she asked, determined to keep her voice light and not let him know her heart was breaking.

"No," Rick said diffidently. "I've got some names, but it's too soon to tell if anyone will work out."

The news should have pleased her, at least offered her some relief from the guilt she'd been feeling; it did just the opposite, made her realize how possessive she felt about the job—and him—and how much she wanted both back.

It had only been a little over two months since she had last seen him, yet it felt like an eternity. Until she'd left him, she hadn't realized it was possible for her to miss another human being quite that much. And she still didn't know what to do with the wealth of feelings she had inside of her. She only knew she had regrets about leaving Kentucky, and most particularly about leaving him. There wasn't a day went by that she didn't wonder what might have developed between them had she chosen to stay on in Kentucky, had she chosen to work by his side, as he had wanted her to. And since coming back, those doubts and feelings had escalated ten-fold. And yet she was afraid to say anything, afraid to make an overture toward him or put him on the spot, for fear of embarrassing and humiliating them both and making things even more awkward than they were at this moment. He had been so disappointed in her when she'd left. She knew from her abrupt conversations with him on the phone he still felt that way, deep down. All she could do now was make small talk—to salvage the moment—and then get out of there as soon as she could. "So... how's your family?"

"Everyone's fine," he reassured her softly, his intent look every bit as honest as his voice.

"Good."

His brow rose.

"I care about them. You know that."

He acknowledged that with a brief nod. After a moment, he replied in a husky voice, "They care about you, too." He paused a beat. "And they miss you."

He'd said they, not him. Yet Hilary's heart was suddenly beating so loudly she could hear it. It was now or never. Take the plunge or spend the rest of her life wondering. "And what about you?" she asked softly, needing and wanting to know how he felt deep down. Not the others—not now—just him.

His silver eyes darkened. He closed the distance between them cautiously. "Do you even have to ask?" he said hoarsely. "Hell, yes, I missed you, every minute of every day."

She blinked back tears of happiness at the words she had so longed to hear. "Oh, Rick, I missed you, too," she confessed emotionally.

They met in each other's arms. For long minutes he held her against him. To Hilary, nothing had ever felt so good or so right. "I thought when you left it would be easy to go on," he confessed gruffly after a minute, stroking her hair. "It hasn't been."

"I thought so, too," she admitted in a trembling voice. Unable to get enough of him, she lifted her face to his. And in that moment the truth hit her with blinding clarity. There would never be another man she would love as much or as deeply as Rick. Knowing that, their different goals in life no longer seemed to matter. What counted was that they be together, that they somehow find a way.

He studied her briefly, his eyes lovingly caressing her face. Slowly, his expression changed. She could tell he was trying to understand her, to read what was in her heart and her mind. His brow furrowing, he said, "I thought returning to Boston, your job there, was what you wanted."

Their two months apart had given Hilary time to do some soul-searching of her own. "I thought so, too, Rick, and it was exciting at first. But now that I've proved myself again and the novelty of being back home has worn off—" she shook her head, knowing she had to be honest with him or regret it the rest of her life "—I'm beginning to see no matter how much